Murder

at the Movies

Janice Detrie

Murder at the Movies
Copyright © 2025 by Janice Detrie

ISBN: 978-0-9987342-4-8

Printed in the United States of America

This is a work of fiction. Names, characters, places, and incidents are either a product of the author's imagination or are used fictitiously. Any resemblance to actual events, or persons or locales, living or dead, is purely coincidental.

Published by
Janice Detrie

Cover design by Eric Labacz
www.labaczdesign.com

Prologue

I laid the trap weeks ago. All it took was an email with the subject line "Interested in writing for the Milwaukee Post?"

A free movie ticket in exchange for a film review. She'd get a byline in the Arts and Culture section and maybe even more commissions. A follow up letter spelled it all out. Victoria Fitzgerald was so vain she never questioned why the second largest newspaper in the state would pluck her out of thin air and as for her opinion.

The movie itself sealed the deal—an exclusive showing of Moon Rise over the Moor. *Exclusive mostly because only about three people in all of Crawford would be actually willing to sit through a three-hour period piece.*

Victoria was obsessed with exclusivity. When she left town, she thought her new life would be bright lights and big city adventure. The latest plays on Broadway, book signings at the Strand, concerts at Lincoln Center. And for a few years, it seemed like she made it out.

Then last year her father needed help with the custom-made furniture business, so here she is back in Crawford. Helping the wealthy clients select expensive unique office furniture. She may wear a mask of gentility with them. But I know how truly ugly she is, how hateful and cruel with her snide remarks and humiliating put-downs.

Going to a movie always brought me back to myself after the worst of her abuse. The calm you feel in the absolute dark before the previews flick on. How time stops when you watch a good car chase. The rush of adrenaline that floods your body when the killer finally corners his victim.

Today I have cornered mine. Payback has been a long time in coming but now it's near. I can taste victory, butter flavored and salty.

Victoria sits in the exact center seat, notepad in hand, as the lights start to fade. Almost no one is here except for the two of us. The only movement flickers on the screen. She's so focused she doesn't notice me, hunched down behind her, waiting for terrifying storm scene. Earsplitting thunder cracks over the speakers, the wind rages.

It's loud enough to wake the dead.

chapter one
Don't Call Me Maybe

Vlad Chomsky tried to remember when a phone call from his ex-wife, Maria filled him with anything resembling joy and tranquility, but he drew a complete blank. Usually her phone calls brought frustration and misery. Today was no exception.

"Where the hell are you? I've been trying to reach you for over an hour. My calls went directly to voice mail." Her shrill voice produced the same sensation as the squeal of a fax machine. "Don't you ever check your calls?"

Vlad thought, *not when I see your name in the call log.* Instead he said, "I was walking on the Interurban Trail with Gaston. I'm dog-sitting while Sandra plays Mahjong. What's up?" he tugged nervously at his well-trimmed mustache. Conversations with Maria were usually stressful.

The only thing Sandra Tooksbury, his elderly landlady, loved more than solving crimes was Mahjong. She said it sharpened her observation skills with the intense play and keeping one step ahead of her opponents with her strategic moves was like tracking down a suspect before her nemesis, Detective Johnson, took over the case.

"Why didn't Mrs. Tooksbury take her fat cantankerous poodle along? She hauls him everywhere else."

He raked his fingers through his thinning hair, thinking of an appropriate response to her belligerent question. "For some reason, the other ladies asked her to leave him at home. Claimed he was too distracting."

"I can't imagine how anyone could make such an outrageous statement as that." Maria's voice dripped with sarcasm. Vlad could feel her eyes rolling over the cell phone connection. "Especially since he's endowed with innate crime solving abilities," she added.

"Whether you believe it's his intuition or coincidence, Gaston brought down the guilty parties in several high-profile cases." Vlad gazed affectionately at the sleeping poodle snuggled up on his loveseat, his curly head resting peacefully on grey paws. "He saved me twice."

"You wouldn't have needed saving at all if you weren't caught up in your landlady's delusions of playing detective. I can't believe a sensible woman like Beatrice Krup gets sucked in by her crazy capers. But she did get engaged to you, so she must be gullible."

Vlad cut her off before she could continue with her familiar rants about his new fiancée and his lifestyle choices. "At any rate, Sandra left him with me and we went for a walk. You still haven't told me why you called."

"Can you pick up Erin at six? She's working at the Classic this afternoon. I'm meeting with some buyers at five. They want to write an offer on the house I showed them yesterday. Some of us don't get weekends and summers off."

Vlad ignored the dig at his teaching job at Crawford College. Even when they were married, Maria's dissatisfaction with his academic career was apparent. She disparaged the afternoon teas with the other faculty wives as boring. Instead, she took up bowling, where she met Al, her first extramarital fling. She progressed to her own career in real estate and a long-term relationship with Gordy, her boss.

"No problem. What about the other two kids?"

Sometimes Maria allowed Nicholas, age eleven, to babysit Kaitlyn, age five, for a short period of time, with uneven results. Kaitlyn rebelled when her big brother tried to control her, yelling "you're not the boss of me!"

"They're at Nettie's house, playing with Liam. She said they could stay for supper."

"I'll gladly pick Erin up. Gives me a chance to catch up with what's happening with her. When she's trapped in the car, she's forced to talk to me."

"Hah!' Maria snorted. "All she talks about is buying a car. Now that she's turned sixteen, she's obsessed with getting her license and her own wheels."

"At least she's working after school at the movie theater and earning her own money to buy one." Vlad puffed out his chest. "She's not asking for a handout!"

"She has to work. You barely make enough for child support and your tiny apartment. And I'm just getting started in the real estate business."

Maria still knew how to deflate his ego, but Vlad refused to let her upset him. "I'm proud she's taken the initiative to go after what she wants. She's ambitious, like her mother."

"I suppose you're right." Maria's voice softened. "Remember, she's done at six. Park behind the theater. She should be out shortly."

"Will do. Gaston will come with. He'll be happy to see her, too."

At the sound of his name, Gaston glanced up, his bright eyes fixed on the vest pocket where Vlad kept the treats. He gave a hopeful yip and rose to a sitting posture. The fly-away fur on his floppy ears gave him the frowsy look of a bar fly. When the first yip didn't produce the desired results, he yipped a little louder, then jumped to the floor. His briskly wagging tail sent ripples down his low hanging tummy. Still, Vlad ignored him, intent on ending the call with Maria.

"Good luck with the offer. I'll take Erin to Cullen's Dairy for supper."

Just as he rang off, Vlad felt a cold nose against his ankle.

"Yikes! What's wrong with you?" Vlad reached down to pat the little dog's head..

The pooch whined like a baby wanting attention. He pawed at Vlad's pant leg, still eyeing the vest pocket. The khaki fishing vest was ideal for walks in the park with Gaston and the kids. One pocket was for Gaston's treat, another for Sour Patch Kids, and still another to hold his antacids. A wad of Kleenex filled the fourth.

"Sit!" Vlad commanded in his best drill sergeant voice. Not only did Gaston sit, he rolled on his back, stomach up, with four paws waving in the air. He wiggled to and fro, begging pathetically.

Vlad laughed and gave him a brisk tummy rub. "You rascal! I'll give you a Pork Comps. But you need to behave when we pick up Erin before you get another."

Chapter Two
A Mostly Ghostly Tale

Erin glanced at the clock behind her. Only two o'clock. Still four hours to go. Time dragged after the busy matinee rush of ticket selling, filling popcorn bags, taking soda and candy orders. Working behind the counter at the small three-screen theater meant you did everything. The ticket booth at the entrance was inhabited by a female mannequin in a glamourous blonde wig and a red sequined blouse. Movie goers came through the red carpeted lobby past gigantic posters of coming attractions to the concession counter, where Erin and her fellow worker, Barb, filled orders under the watchful eye of Mark Hoffman, their boss. Always ready to pitch in when the crowds grew too large, he filled the soda machine canisters and hauled in big boxes of candy—all the tasks that required strong arms and back. Despite his shaggy hair and beard badly in need of a trim, Mark was meticulous when it came to serving customers.

After the initial flurry of customers, he asked, "Will one of you check how many people are in *Moon Rise Over the Moor*?"

There had to be at least three people before they'd show an unpopular movie. The projectionist, Henry Radke, declared it wasn't worth the bother of maintaining three screens if one of them was to a nearly empty theater. The magic number was three.

Erin tucked her dark, curly ponytail back into her scrunchie and tightened it. Since she started working part time, she let her hair grow back and stopped wearing heavy black eyeliner and purple lipstick. With her freshly scrubbed face and just a bit of lip gloss, she looked like a normal teen, highly employable and trustworthy.

Mark's request hung in the air. She and Barb stared at each other, neither one wanting to travel down the dimly lit hall to open the door of the dark theater. Until the coming attractions lit up the screen, all-encompassing darkness dominated the room. In the obscure light, patrons could barely make out the grey upholstered seats as they fumbled their way. The midnight blue walls with the felt soundproofing stripes absorbed light as well as sound. The small flickering exit light was the only beacon in the gloom.

Barb, a sturdy, squat woman, suddenly busied herself restocking the candy in the glass counter. Her salt and pepper hair confined on the side by a silver barrette bounced with the vigor of her movements. Erin stood by, helplessly studying the lobby for an excuse not to do the check. Barb didn't often play the seniority card, but the conversation with Henry yesterday had spooked them both.

Mark had been in his office setting up the website for the upcoming attractions. Barb was putting oil in the popcorn machine, getting ready to fill the black basket with kernels. Soon the lobby would be filled with the delicious aroma of the popped corn. Erin was sorting bags of M and M's, boxes of Milk Duds and Mike and Ike's, arranging them invitingly on the shelf. A Pixar movie was the family feature. The boxes of overpriced candy would fly off the shelves, appeasing the noisy children clamoring for treats. Henry leaned against the soda fountain watching them work, assiduously chomping on some gummy bears.

Suddenly he blurted out. "I saw him again last night."

Barb studiously ignored him, but Erin, being the newbie, asked, "Saw who, Mr. Radke?"

Henry stared down at his grimy fingernails, which tempted Erin to suggest a visit to the manicure shop down the street. The sweet Asian woman that ran it would have a field day with his nails. The silence lasted so long, she thought he didn't hear her question. She asked again, a little louder.

"Who did you see last night?"

Henry pushed his thinning hair back from his high forehead, and sucked his cheek, twisting his mouth into a lopsided grimace. "First the old projection room got really cold. I felt a chill go down my back. I figured Mark turned up the air conditioning. I felt like someone was watching me. I turned to see if Mark came in. Then I saw him—the man in the tan suit."

"Who's the man in the tan suit?" Erin's brown eyes widened in alarm.

Before Henry could answer, Barb let out a loud rush of air. "Henry Radke, don't fill her head with your nonsense, you jackass."

"It's not nonsense." Henry narrowed his eyes as he drew his lips into a tight frown. "I saw him standing on the little balcony that overlooks the back of the old theater. Plain as I see you standing here."

Erin dropped the green box of candy, and gawked at Henry. "Is it a ghost?"

Barb scoffed, "It's a story that Henry makes up for attention, from sitting alone too long in dark rooms, watching the same movies over and over. He has to walk past old cut outs of characters from past movies. It sparks his imagination."

"I'm not the only one that's seen him. Bob, the projectionist before me, saw him, too." Henry jabbed his finger at her. "You know Bob said he saw him."

"Bob was a few bricks short of a load. I'm starting to think you're a little wacky too."

"If I'm so wacky, why do you always send the new girls up to Mark's office when you need to get ahold of him?"

Erin stared at Barb with dawning recognition of the few times she sent her up the stairs on an errand. The faded, blood red carpet with gold Art Deco designs emitted a musty smell as she stomped up the steps, careful not to trip on the treads. In the hallway, she sidled past the lower half of the mannequin with its bare legs, and the crumpled standup figures of old movie actors, expecting a mouse, or worse still a rat, to come scurrying over her foot. She shivered at the thought of a ghost, not a rat.

Barb protested. "My knees are bad; I can't take those stairs like I could when I was younger."

Henry snorted. "I think you're scared you might meet the man in the tan suit in one of the dark crannies."

"No. I'm afraid I might trip on some of that junk Mark's got stashed up there. Mannequin torsos, old projectors, stacks of empty reels, boxes of old box office receipts. I try not to think of the fire hazards."

"You try not to think of a guy coming back from the dead. There are more than a few secrets in this old theater. I know what I saw. A man in a glowing tan suit. When I stood up, he vanished."

"Why don't you take a hint and do the same?" Barb faced him, hands on hips. "We got work to do. The Saturday afternoon crowd is always the biggest."

Erin hurriedly ducked down and picked up the scattered boxes. When she stood up, Henry was gone. The only sound was the popcorn maker exploding the hard kernels.

"Is he for real?" Erin's voice quivered as she turned to stacking the soda cups.

"Nah. Henry's a big blow hard. He likes to creep out the high school kids with his cock and bull stories. Ask Mark if he's ever seen a ghost. He practically lives in this place."

Erin considered her boss's reaction if she asked him such a question. He'd probably think she was an idiot. The discussion with Henry felt like the beginning of a Scooby Doo cartoon, with her being cast as Daphne. She gave her head a little shake. "I'll take a pass."

Now Mark stood there in the lobby, hands on hips, waiting for one of them to acknowledge he spoke. He cleared his throat and asked again, "Ahem. One of you gals want to check the big screen theater?"

"I should probably watch the popcorn. We get complaints if it's burned," Barb said.

Erin sighed. "I'll go, Mr. Hoffman. Be right back."

She lingered for a moment in the brightly lit lobby, hoping for a rush of latecomers that would necessitate her help at the counter. No such luck. She reluctantly turned toward the shadowy hallway, playing a little trivia game in her head. Mark had painted famous lines from classic movies on the long wall to the old theater, and she read them as she loitered in the passage, trying to identify the subsequent movie. *We're not in Kansas anymore.* "Easy," she whispered to herself. "The Wizard of Oz." *You're not too old to be young.* "Not so easy. I haven't a clue." The most ominous quote was above the door to the theater. *It's a trap!* Mark told her the line from *Star Wars* was his way of warning unsuspecting movie goers about the drop down into the dark room. The disclaimer below it said, *NO. Really. Watch your step.*

Playing the game kept Erin from thinking about the man in the tan suit. She slowly pushed open the door and peeked inside. She gave her eyes a few seconds to adjust to the dim light. She counted a couple down in front and one woman smack dab in the middle of the theater. A long-haired man near the aisle munched a giant bag of popcorn. A head popped up in the back row—too far away for her to tell male or female.

Mark stood waiting by the refreshment stand as she scurried back. "I counted five people," Erin said, a little breathless from running down the hall.

"I'll go tell Henry to start the previews. We'll show the movie." He pivoted and headed up the stairs.

Barb took one look at Erin's pale face and patted her shoulder. "Forget what Henry said. He's kidding around. There's no ghost haunting this movie theater. I've been working here for fifteen years. The scariest thing I saw was when the men's toilet got clogged and overflowed. Now that's a sight I never want to see again."

chapter Three
The Final Exit

The four o'clock showing of the Pixar movie kept Erin and Barb hustling. Mark pitched in with the ticket selling while they worked the counter. Because it was the first weekend of the show, more parents and kids came to the second matinee than usual. Candy and soft drinks flew off the shelves. Barb refilled the popcorn maker three times. Erin's brunette hair escaped from the ponytail and she was too busy to tuck it back in. Even the action film had more people attending in the late afternoon. The cold autumn drizzle drove people inside. What better place to be than at the movies? Plus Ryan Gosling, the big star, always drew a big crowd, no matter if he appeared in a comedy, romance, or adventure film.

Finally, there was a lull. Erin felt so tired, she wanted to sink onto the big carton emptied of plastic cups and rest her feet. She let out a big puff of air and blew the straggles of hair away from her perspiring face.

"I'm taking care of this mess before something gets ground into the carpet," Mark said as he went to the small janitor's closet and grabbed a vacuum cleaner. He did a quick sweep of the lobby, sucking up the detritus of popcorn kernels, crushed M and M's, and assorted candies.

Then he peered at his watch. "*Moon Rise Over the Moors* is about to let out. Erin, would you please do a spot check of the theater? Pick up any trash. Let me know if I need to vacuum in there, too."

Erin opened her mouth to protest, then snapped it shut. No sense in complaining when Mark was doing all the heavy lifting. She glanced over at Barb, who sprayed the dirty counter with a cleaner and wiped away the spills. She had worked just as hard as Erin and was probably three times her age. Barb's once clean shirt had grease stains from squirting fake butter on the popcorn, sparing Erin that messy job. Erin felt a surge of gratitude for the older lady.

Checking out the emptying theater was much easier than doing the gross clean up.

"Sure, Mr. Hoffman. I'll be glad to." She stepped into the lobby, careful to avoid the obstacle course of crushed candy. The space behind the counter became extremely hot due to the continual popping of the corn. The cooler air in the lobby provided a welcome relief.

Erin once again corralled the stray locks of hair into the purple scrunchie. Her hair was finally long enough to fit into a pony tail. No more black hair dye and goth clothes, although she still listened to the emo music. When her parents split up, she felt like it had been her fault. Angst filled lyrics spoke to her soul and made her feel rebellious. She pushed all their buttons, especially her mom's. Maria was just too easy to light up. When she observed how upset her younger siblings were, especially her brother, Nicholas, she decided to be part of the solution, since her family seemed to have enough problems. Working part time at the aquatic center in the summer and now at the Classic meant more than earning money for a car. It meant independence. The car would be her ticket to adventure.

Mark and Barb were both so engrossed in cleaning up, they didn't notice Erin taking out her phone and checking her texts. Her BFF Jillian sent her four messages, telling her what she'd missed at Riverview Park. Alex, a boy she kind of liked, had been there asking about her. A smile crept across her face thinking about him and his awkward flirting. He was so shy, but very cute in an adorably bumbling way. The final text was from her dad. He'd be waiting on Fourth Street at six. She could count on a trip to Cullen's Dairy for supper.

In spite of Barb's comments downplaying Henry's spook sighting, Erin still felt uneasy. The theater was old. Auntie Sandra remembered live performances on the stage back in the day when she was touring with her dog act, and she was older than dirt. Some restless spirits might hang around—look at the Phantom of the Opera. Who was the man in the tan suit anyway?

Soon the few people who sat through the entire three-hour movie started wandering out of the old theater. The bougie couple from up front bickered in a heated argument. "You're wrong," the woman declared, flipping her long, dark hair back with a bejeweled hand, her diamond tennis bracelet glittering despite the dim light. "Maeve's dilemma had more to do with her need to hold herself apart, not to her struggle as an artist. Her inner conflict overwhelmed her."

The balding male shook his head. "When Nigel denounced her painting, his rejection brought about her demise. It was Nigel's fault."

"How would you know?" his companion argued. "You missed the climax when you went to the men's room."

"I could hear the noisy storm and the screaming from the lobby," he said with a wave of dismissal.

Erin wondered at the type of patron who could react so passionately about a boring movie. She loitered as they passed her by. Sporting a ponytail that caused her a twinge of envy, the thirty something loner with the long hair followed close behind the clamorous couple. His hands were shoved deep in the pockets of his barn jacket. The pungent odor of greasy popcorn overpowered the aroma of his woodsy aftershave. A few dribbles dotted the tan canvas jacket. As he passed, he nodded curtly at her.

The other two movie goers must be the diehards who watched every second of the credits. Erin identified a few more movie quotes as she strolled down the hall. *"E. T. phone home." No stretch there. "To Infinity and beyond." Of course,* Toy Story *"My momma always said life was like a box of chocolates. You never know what you're gonna get." Not sure about that one.*

When she pushed open the door, the credits from the songs performed in the movie flashed by. Not a single song she recognized. Her eyes took a moment to adjust to the dim light. Then the large A from Annapurna Pictures and the Roman numeral date faded from the screen. Only the woman in the center row remained. Her head was down. The movie was so boring it had put her in a sound sleep. Erin totally understood how this crappy arthouse film was a big snooze fest. She wondered why Mark continued to show these types of movies. Guess you had to take the good with the bad sometimes.

The lights came on, Still the woman didn't stir. Her chin rested on her chest. Her immaculately styled blonde hair covered her face like a wedding veil. Her black leather coat was draped over the back of her seat. Even Erin could tell it was expensive by how velvet-like the leather lay, not stiff like her bomber jacket. One pale white hand lay on the seat beside her, fingers turned upwards.

Erin inched her way down the middle of the row of empty seats. The cloying odor of flowery perfume overpowered the stale popcorn smell. As she drew nearer, she saw the plastic soda cup lying at the woman's feet, the spilled soda forming a small lake under her high heeled boots. *Great!* She thought. *Someone will have to clean that up before the evening showing!*

Erin cleared her throat with a loud "Ahem," not wanting to startle her awake. No response from the silent figure. The only sound was the loud buzzing of some bees that were hovering behind the woman. *How did those bees get in? Did Barb leave the door to the alley open again?* Bees always swarmed around the dumpster, lured by the sticky spills. *Honestly she can be so careless when she needs a smoke.*

One particularly aggressive bee dive-bombed Erin. "Go away, bee," she yelped. Her arm swung wildly like a weathervane in a hurricane. The buzzing grew louder as the bee hovered above her ear. A panicked swat made the bee disappear. Surprisingly the woman continued sleeping through the disturbance.

"Madam, please wake up. I'm sorry. The movie is over," she said softly. She reached down to give her shoulder a gentle shake. When she touched the woman, her body toppled onto the armrest, and her head jerked back. The veil of blond hair fell away to reveal one glassy eye and one angry red eye swollen to a narrow slit. Purple bulging lips gaped open in a silent scream. Half of her face had ballooned into a crimson fright mask, a mutant distortion of what had once been a pretty face. Whatever horrors she felt in her last moments were forever entombed within her still body.

Erin stood mesmerized by the nightmare face until she noticed a thin trickle of vomit sliding down the woman's chin. The sour smell assaulted her nostrils and she fought the urge to puke. "Oh my God! She's dead!" She pivoted, slipping on the spilled soda. Her hands grasped an empty seat to prevent herself from pitching facedown. Pulling herself upright, she scrambled over the row of seats. The sprint up the empty aisle seemed to last forever. Blind terror catapulted her into the bright lights of the lobby away from the nightmarish scene.

Chapter Four
A Damsel's Demise

The cold rain altered Vlad's plans to grade papers while waiting for Erin in the car. Despite Gaston's pathetic whine, he refused to surrender to his pleading. "No, you can't come into the theater. You need to stay in the car. Besides, you know how you hate to get your paws wet."

The slight drizzle turned into steady rain. The rhythmic beat on the car roof drowned out the dog's protests. Gaston gave up and hunkered down in the back. Vlad reached under the driver's seat for a small umbrella and plodded down the street into the theater lobby. He dodged a dark-haired bearded man furiously running the vacuum cleaner up and down the entry, past the floor to ceiling posters of coming attractions. His Justice League t-shirt hung loosely over faded blue jeans.

Vlad watched him make a few passes back and forth before he shouted above the roar of the machine, "I'm Vlad Chomsky, here to pick up my daughter, Erin" He craned his neck looking for her in the concessions counter, but only the frazzled-looking older woman stared back at him.

"She should be out any minute. I'm Mark Hoffman, her boss," the man said, shutting off the vacuum. "She just went in to check on the condition of the theater. Shouldn't need much clean up. Only a small crowd. Not like the Disney film with all the kiddos."

"Or the action flick starring Ryan Gosling," Barb added. "We were running around like rats on a sinking ship."

Mark tossed her an annoyed look. "It was busier than usual with the bad weather, but it wasn't as bad as all that."

"I didn't know if I was coming or going for a while." Barb protested. "That's what happens when you have to take tickets and serve the snacks."

"It's how I manage to keep our ticket prices low," Mark said. "They have more people working at the AMC in Windsor

Hills, but it costs nearly fifty bucks for two people to go to the movies and get popcorn and a soda at the mall."

"Crawford appreciates the bargain prices," Vlad said. "And Erin appreciates the chance to make some money on the weekends."

"She's a good worker. One of the best of all the high school kids I've hired over the years."

"The rain is coming down fairly heavy so I dashed in with an umbrella." Vlad held up a compact travel umbrella in a black sheath. "I figured she might need a little protection from the weather."

The large door leading into the old, refurbished theater banged open. A shrill scream, followed by pounding footsteps startled both men.

"What the hell?" Mark blurted out.

"It sounds like Erin!" Vlad ditched the umbrella on the counter and hustled toward the dim corridor. Mark dropped the vacuum handle and followed close on his heels.

Vlad knew something horrible had happened when he caught sight of Erin charging toward him. The whites of her wild eyes reminded him of the blind terror of stampeding pronghorn sheep. She'd lost the scrunchie in her mad panic to flee the theater and her tangled hair flew about her ashen face. He flung open his arms to catch her as she stumbled in her haste to get to safety. She sobbed incoherently for a few seconds, burying her face in his chest.

Finally she managed to choke out a few words. "A dead woman in the theater. Something wrong with her face. It's horrible."

"Call 911! I'll check her out," Mark said as he sprinted past them down the long hallway.

Vlad grabbed his cell phone out of his coat pocket and dialed the emergency number. "Send an ambulance to Classic Cinema. A woman has collapsed in the old theater."

"She's dead," Erin wailed. "She looks beyond help."

Vlad held the trembling girl tightly. "Are you sure she's dead?" he softly asked.

"Yes, I'm sure." Her breath came in hiccups as her shoulders jerked. "She didn't move when I tried to wake her up.

Her one eye was swollen shut. Her face was all red and puffy. And her lips, they were big and purple, total freak out."

"I know CPR. Maybe I should go and check. Give Mark a hand."

"I can't go back in there. I just can't." Erin squeezed her eyes tightly shut. Her face crumpled like a punctured tire. "Please don't make me."

Barb appeared, her forehead knotted with concern. "What's going on?" She clutched her hands to her chest. "I heard screaming."

"Erin said a woman died in the theater. Mark went to check on her." Vlad placed his hands gently on Erin's shoulders and looked squarely in her face. "I'd like to go check on the woman. I've had some experience with dead... with this kind of thing. Do you think you can stay here in the lobby with…? He glanced at the woman standing nearby.

"Barb," she prompted.

"With Barb while I give Mark a hand?"

"Come here, darlin', and I'll get you a Sprite. Something cold to calm your nerves." She tossed her flabby arm across Erin's trembling shoulders and drew her near to her substantial bosom. "Let's go back to the concessions stand and find you a drink."

"OK." Erin sniffled. "I could use a drink."

Vlad shot a grateful look at the older woman. "Thanks, Barb. I'll be right back."

As he trudged past the movie quotes on the walls, Vlad could almost hear the frenetic chords that introduced a *Twilight Zone* episode. His jangling nerves throbbed in lock step with the discordant rhythms inside his head. The words *It's a Trap* above the entrance only made the foreboding feeling worse. He shoved open the door, stumbling on the uneven floor. In the center of a row of empty seats, Mark was bent over a still figure lying in a pool of spilled soda. His body filled the narrow space between the seats and blocked Vlad's view of the woman.

The manager tugged on the ankle of her stiletto heeled boots as he maneuvered her toward the aisle. His labored breathing echoed in the hollow space of the empty theater.

Mark cried out to him, "I can't do CPR in such a small area. I need more room. Can you please lend a hand?" He straightened up, then crawled over the seats to reach her head and lift her shoulders.

The woman's head bobbled sideways and her blond hair fanned out below her. As Vlad drew near, he got a good look at the deformed facial features on half of her face, one eye swollen shut, lips puffed up like a Peeps heated in a microwave, just like Erin had described. The raised red blotches contrasted with the pretty cheekbones and bold eye make-up on the untouched half. His jaw dropped as he assessed her damaged face. "What the hell happened to her?"

Mark gave a curt nod in the direction of the woman's boots. "Please grab her feet?"

Vlad grasped her slippery boots trying to avoid being stabbed by the sharp heels. Together they lifted her into the aisle, carefully laying her down. Immediately, the manager began administering CPR. The heel of one hand on top of the body, pressed down stiffly, with the other firmly on top. Vlad heard him humming "Staying Alive" as he pumped up and down vigorously. Under her now vacant seat, a bee circled round the puddle of sticky soda, while another alighted on a squished Milk Dud.

After several minutes of quick compressions, Mark exclaimed, "She's not breathing. It looks like the bees stung her. I can see the welts where the stinger penetrated." He pumped even harder.

"God! She must have a severe allergy to bee stings!"

A bead of sweat appeared on Mark's forehead as he increased the downward thrusts. "Her lips are so swollen I can't do a rescue breath."

"Do you want me to give you a break? I've been trained in CPR."

"Nope. I'm good. I hope the paramedics get here soon. They are better equipped to deal with this." He continued the steady pushes.

"You got a defibrillator somewhere? That'd be the next step."

"Unfortunately, no. But you better believe I will in the future," Mark muttered through gritted teeth.

A patch of bright light streamed in when the outside door opened and two paramedics rushed in. A burly Sumo type was in the lead, followed by an angular companion pushing the stretcher. Vlad recognized them as the same two men who rescued him after the attack on Tivoli Island by the ruthless killer trying to scare him off during the poisoned pie case last summer.

The lead man recognized him, too. "Dr. Chomsky, you're looking better than the last time we saw you." Vlad scooted out of the way to let them pass. They wheeled the stretcher past the rows of seats as Mark desperately tried to revive her.

"We'll take it from here," the lead EMT said. "We have a defib in the wagon."

The men expertly lifted the woman onto the stretcher. The gangly one pulled a mask out and fitted it over the woman's face. The flow of oxygen began immediately, but there was no change in her chest movement. Her hands hung limply at her side, the heels of her boots aimed like daggers at the hulking paramedic as he strapped her down.

"Got any idea who she is? Where's her identification?"

Mark scurried back to her seat and knelt down in the sticky mess to check around.

"Nothing here. No purse. Just her coat." He handed the Ichabod Crane look-alike her leather cloak. "But I've seen her before around town. Her name's Victoria Fitzgerald. Her dad owns the custom furniture business."

"Well, she's Jane Doe until we get a positive ID," he remarked over his shoulder as he shoved the stretcher up the aisle.

As the paramedic team whisked her out of the dark theater, Mark and Vlad watched them leave in shocked silence. Finally, their eyes met and Vlad spoke. "Hopefully, they have the proper equipment to revive her."

Mark wiped his brow with the back of his hand. "I couldn't find a pulse. She was already starting to turn cold. But I gave her my best shot." His shoulders slumped forward and he slowly shook his head.

"Sometimes life imitates art" Vlad reflected. "Death comes when you least expect it—at a matinee on a rainy Sunday afternoon."

Chapter Five
A Bewildering Discovery

It was a hell of a way to spend a Sunday afternoon. Vlad offered the umbrella to Erin as they walked into the fall rain. She shook her head no and let the rain wash over her tear-stained face. Jamming her hands in the pockets of her leather bomber jacket, she walked wordlessly to the car, hunched over like an old woman. Tears fell again as she slid into the passenger seat. Alarmed by her shaking shoulders, Gaston jumped over the console and onto her lap. He licked the teardrops from her face with a low-throated little whine. The stricken girl flung her arms around him and held him tightly.

"Do you want to talk about it?" Vlad asked.

Erin shook her head.

"Should we get something to eat? We can go to a drive through or Collin's Dairy," he offered.

"I'm not very hungry."

Vlad placed a comforting hand on her shoulder then moved to gently rub the back of her neck. He pushed aside her wet hair. The delicate neck bones felt so vulnerable. "What would you like to do?"

"I'd like to talk to Auntie Sandra. She just found that Marco guy dead at the bottom of the stairs. She'll understand."

***

If Sandra Tooksbury was surprised to see the dripping teen when she opened her door, her face didn't give any clue to her bewilderment. When she saw her visitors, she ran her fingers through her tousled red hair, with a hint of grey roots. A smudge of Starlet Red lipstick showed on her teeth when she smiled warmly at the soggy trio. As she stepped back to let them in, the wide legs of her purple satin jumpsuits swished in rhythm with the clanking strands of crystal beads around her neck.

Gaston only left Erin's side in the entry way to shake the rain drops from his fur. Vlad extended the umbrella in front as a shield against the wet onslaught, then placed it on the tiled floor to drip dry before they entered Sandra's apartment.

"May we come in?" he asked. "Erin really needs to talk to you. Something terrible happened this afternoon at the movie theater."

"Of course, dearie. Let me take your wet things." Sandra held out her hands to Erin as she shrugged off her jacket and kicked off her wet shoes. The girl's pant legs were soaked through and her white no show socks had a black tint from the shoes' black dye. The pale green hoodie was the only dry spot on her. Erin wrapped her arms around herself and shivered in the hallway.

After Sandra tossed the jacket on the hall tree, she inspected the bedraggled girl from head to toes. "You look as if you could use a hot bath and some dry clothes, and then a cup of my special hot chocolate. Why don't you come with me and I'll run some hot water in the tub?" She slipped her arm around the quivering teen and guided her toward the bathroom. "I'll throw your wet clothes into the dryer. You can borrow my robe until they dry. You'll be toasty in no time. Then we can talk."

Gaston trailed behind the two, yipping his encouragement to Erin as he loped in circles around her. He stopped to give her hand her hand a sloppy lick. The girl paused to ruffle the fur on his head.

"That's a good boy, Gaston." Sandra said to the dog. "We'll take care of whatever ails this girl."

Vlad threw her a grateful look as he lined up both his and Erin's shoes neatly on the multi-colored rag rug near the door. He hung his coat on the open peg on the hall tree and padded in his stocking feet over to the kitchen. "Should I make us a pot of coffee?"

"That would be lovely." Sandra voice drifted from the bathroom retreat. "Could you please put a cup of water in the microwave for two minutes? I'll be out shortly to make Erin some hot chocolate."

Vlad surveyed the cupboard where Sandra usually kept the ground coffee. All he saw was a black and brown bag with shiny gold lightning strikes separating the black on the top from the gold bottom. A skull and crossbones logo was smack dab in the center of the bag, encircled by the wording *The Death by Coffee Co.*

Below it read: Warning: The World's Strongest Coffee.

With more than slight apprehension, he opened the bag and sniffed. A burnt toast smell floated up to his nostrils. When he peered into the bag, it looked like ordinary coffee, dark brown and granular. The drip coffee maker stood nearby on the counter. He filled the glass coffee pot with tap water—at least that was safe—and poured it in the reservoir. He was scooping the coffee into the filter basket when Sandra entered.

"Are you trying to make a statement with this new coffee brand?" Vlad arched his eyebrow. "Offer it up to potential suspects?"

"No, dearie. Nothing sinister like that." Sandra took out the canister of sugar and a box of cocoa powder and began mixing the two together in a large measuring cup with a pinch of salt. "It was free at the food pantry. Apparently, it wasn't a big seller at the grocery store. Free is free, after all, when you're on a fixed income."

"I was starting to worry that sleuthing was leading you to the dark side." Vlad flipped the switch and the coffee began dripping slowly into the pot. "Thank you for comforting Erin. I didn't know what else to do when she asked to see you. She's had a hell of a shock."

"So she said. She tried to describe the dead woman. Sounded ghastly. Worse that finding Marco." She gave a little shake of her head at the memory of finding the second victim of the pickleball killer, collapsed at the bottom of a deserted stairwell at the fitness center.

"I can't find the words to tell you what a horror she saw. I've seen three dead people, but this woman far and away was the worst sight. I fear my little girl has been thrust into adulthood before she was ready." Vlad gathered three mugs that hung from wooden pegs on a stand. "How will she ever regain her innocence? Once you see a horror like that, you can never unsee it. I hope she doesn't have nightmares. I still have some bad nights."

"Have you considered talking to a therapist? Not only did you stumble upon two murder victims on two separate occasions, you nearly became one yourself. That yoga woman would have shot you without a second thought, if it hadn't been for Gaston." Sandra poured the boiling water into the cocoa mixtures and whipped it with a whisk more and more vigorously as she recalled Vlad's close call.

"Beatrice gave me the same advice. She's been awakened too many times by me shouting at specters. First Donna would materialize in my dreams from a black void, her face all blue, her eyes so dark and lifeless, her mouth in a silent scream, pathetic. She'd reach her bony hands toward me, like she needed me to grab them and pull her into the light. I'd scream at her to go away."

'Oh, dear. That sounds terrible," Sandra clucked sympathetically.

"That's not the worst. Jake Bender sometimes appears, chasing me, with an enormous pickleball racket, with your boa still wrapped around his neck, his tongue protruding and eyes bulging. The sounds he makes in my dream are guttural, not human. I wake up as he's about to strangle me with the boa." Vlad's eyes were squeezed tightly shut. He opened them to flash her a sheepish look. "I finally made an appointment with a therapist. I see her in three weeks."

"Good for you. A real man knows when he needs help and has guts enough to ask for it." Sandra nodded her approval. "Can you grab the half and half from the fridge? I need to whisk some into this hot chocolate to cool it down. Maybe you'd like some for your coffee, too."

The rich odors of coffee and chocolate filled the kitchen. A few sputters, then a loud beep signaled the coffee was done dripping. Erin shuffled out in Sandra's fluffy pink robe, a cotton candy confection belted at the waist. Her face glowed from the steamy bathroom with uncombed hair dangling in wet tangles. Without her dark eye make-up and bright plum lipstick, she looked pale and much younger. The brash teen eager to become independent with her new driving license and future car seemed shrunken and subdued.

"It smells good in here," the girl said. "Hot chocolate sounds great. I kinda O.D.'ed on popcorn today. My shirt stinks like a giant stick of greasy butter."

"Sit down at the table and I'll pour you some of my special concoction. I'm famous for two beverages—my excellent dry martini and my scrumptious hot chocolate." Sandra slid the mug of creamy hot chocolate toward her. Vlad grabbed the coffee pot and poured them both a cupful, before he sat down with the two females. Sandra caught his eye as he examined his daughter closely for signs of trauma. She gave her head a little warning shake, and he turned his attention to Gaston instead.

"Come here, boy. I promised you a puppy treat if you were good." He pulled a nibble out of a pouch in his vest pocket. "Have a few Chomps."

The poodle gobbled them up and sniffed around the floor for more. Finding nothing but linoleum, he gave a disappointed *wuff* and headed for the living room.

Erin inhaled the fragrant steam deeply before wrapping both hands around the mug. Her first sip was cautious. Then she smiled widely and declared. "This is delicious!" She took a bigger swallow. Color started returning to her cheeks as she drained the mug. "May I have some more?"

"Of course, dearie, Sandra said. "I figured one cup wouldn't be enough."

Vlad smiled and said, "The ancient Greeks considered mead the nectar of the Gods, but they never tasted Auntie Sandra's martinis or her hot chocolate."

All three drank for a moment in peaceful silence.

"Dad, I found this in my hoodie when I put it back on." Erin reached into the pocket of Sandra's robe and pulled out a small object wrapped in toilet tissue. She laid it on the table and slowly unwrapped it. Vlad and Sandra leaned in to have a closer look.

Laying in the middle of a white square was a dead bee. Extremely fuzzy golden thorax with six knobby legs. A shiny black and gold abdomen. Translucent gossamer wings. One long slightly bent antenna.

"So, it's a bee," Vlad said after a long pause. "There were several bees in the movie theater."

"I must have killed it when I was swatting at them." Erin brought her face closer to the bee.

"That's to be expected," he said. "Maybe he was dying already. They die after they sting someone."

"I know, Dad, but look closely. It's larger than the bees that hang around the garbage cans in back. Hairier too. And look how long its antenna is. Whatever kind of bee it is, it didn't come in from the back door."

Sandra clapped her hands. "We have a mystery! An unfamiliar bee." She chortled with excitement. "Erin, you just displayed two characteristics of a good detective: an inquiring mind, and keen observation skills."

The elderly woman fixed her bright blue eyes on Vlad, "The apple doesn't fall far from the tree. We may have a new sleuth in the making."

Chapter Six
An Unexpected Visitor

The tall, thin man nervously perched on her couch tapping his right foot. He combed a slender hand through his fine straight ginger hair and gave her a weak smile. Sandra could smell his expensive cologne from her position on the lift chair. Although she seldom used the remote control for the lift, both Vlad and Norm, her handyman, insisted she purchase it, as well as the medical alert pendant she now wore 24/7. "Waste of money," she grumbled as she wrote the exorbitant amount on the check for the recliner. Although she had to admit, the alert device had saved her life when Kristin, the Pickleball Killer, threatened to make her victim number three in the Center for Health and Wellness (CHAW) murders. Susan, the dispatcher for Medi-Alert, sent the police to the center before Kristin could follow through on the threat to suffocate her.

Of course, Gaston held her off until the police arrived. At first his fancy footwork distracted the young killer, who was also the center's custodian. She tried to squirt him in the eyes with the spray bottle of cleaning solution, but he danced out of her reach, all the while barking loudly to attract attention. As Kristin advanced closer to Sandra with the murder weapon, a plastic bag to suffocate her, the crafty poodle attacked from behind knocking the woman down. The police entered the workout room in the nick of time.

Maybe the chair would come in handy someday—if a crazed killer came to her house. She could catapult herself out of the chair, like a human missile and take him down with just the tap of her fingers on the remote. The young man sitting before her didn't appear to be a crazed killer, but you never could tell. Neither had the mousy young custodian. Who knows what evil lurks in the heart of man? Or for that matter, woman? She kept her finger on the remote hidden six the folds of her flouncy patchwork boho skirt just in case.

"How may I help you, young man?" she asked, radiating calm. Looking squarely into his long face, she noted the dark circles under his eyes and the blotchy complexion. Although he was immaculately dressed in a buttoned down, blue pin-striped shirt, and tailored grey trousers, the clothes hung loosely on his gaunt frame. When he crossed his legs, the pant leg lifted up to expose the flesh of his thin ankles above silky dress socks and fine Italian shoes.

Gaston slept on a plush pink pillow next to the young man on the sofa. He opened one eye when the man plopped down, then went back to his morning snooze. Sandra knew it was just subterfuge. The pooch would be at his throat, teeth bared, in a matter of seconds, if the fellow made the slightest wrong move. Gaston was the master of dog deception.

Twisting an onyx ring round and round on his left hand, the man took a deep breath before he spoke. He said in a quivering voice, "As I said when I called, my name is Robert Doering. I am… was engaged to Vicki, Victoria Fitzgerald."

"Ahh. The unfortunate young woman who died at the matinee. I heard she had a terrible allergic reaction to bee stings." Sandra pictured the poor woman's distorted face, as Erin had described it, all puffy with angry red welts.

The man gripped the arm of the sofa with his right hand so tightly the knuckles turned white. "Victoria was extremely allergic to bees." His voice rose an octave as he continued. "Bees were dangerously deadly to her. She almost died from a bee sting when she was a child. That's why she always kept an epi pen in her purse at all times. ALWAYS! Vicki was never without one."

"Why didn't she use it when she got stung in the movie theater? Did she forget to take it with her?"

"That's what's so puzzling," Robert said. "She had one in her purse. I watched her check for it before she left for the show. She walked out the door, purse and epi pen in hand. The theater manager found her purse on top of the recycle bin when he cleaned. No epi pen!" The man pounded his fist on the arm of the sofa. "But Victoria would never leave her purse behind. Never! She carried it with her all the time."

Sandra gazed thoughtfully at her visitor. "Why didn't you accompany her to the movie?"

"Vicki didn't want me to come with her. She had received a free ticket and an invitation from the Arts and Culture editor of the Milwaukee paper to review *Moon Rise Over the Moor* when it opened at the Classic in an exclusive matinee showing. The editor, Timothy McFarland, sent her an email extending the offer. When she accepted—actually she jumped at the chance to write for the newspaper—he sent her the ticket. Actually two tickets. She gave one away to a friend—said she wanted to focus on the movie. I'd be too big of a distraction."

"Had Victoria written reviews for the newspaper before?"

"No, that's why she was so excited about this one. She had an English degree with a Communication Arts minor. She interned with a weekly entertainment magazine in Chicago, the kind that end up in hotel lobbies telling tourists what's happening around town. Her dream was to work for the *Tribune* or some major magazine writing reviews of cultural events."

"How did she end up in Crawford, Wisconsin? We're hardly the epicenter of culture. Frankly, I'm surprised any movie would have an exclusive showing at the Classic Cinema. It's a small undistinguished venue."

"Vicki told me one of the actors attended Crawford University before he moved on to London and the West End. Having the opening here was a big publicity stunt. Apparently British producers don't know much about Wisconsin geography."

"If your fiancé wanted to be a writer in a major city, I don't understand why she chose to live here."

Robert sighed heavily. "Her father owns Fitzgerald's Fine Furniture. They make custom office furniture. He's undergoing chemotherapy for stomach cancer. He needed Vicki to run the business while he's being treated. She sacrificed her aspirations to return home and help out."

"What about you? Did you give up your employment to accompany her?" Sandra's sharp blue eyes scrutinized his reaction.

The thin man twisted his ring so hard it left a red mark on his knuckle. "Unfortunately, I'm between jobs. Vicki's father promised me a position in their marketing department, but that never materialized. I'm able to catch a few freelancing gigs when I can, like a fundraising event for the local animal shelter. I get by. But Vicki is… was… the most important woman in the world to me. That's why I'm here. I heard you were a detective. I'd like to hire you to investigate Vicki's death."

Sandra kept the excitement out of her voice as she calmly replied, "Yes. My associates and I have been able to solve a few cases."

"I'm sorry. I don't have much money to pay you. But I can pawn off Vicki's engagement ring for a down payment." The sad look on his face nearly broke Sandra's heart.

"No worries," she said kindly. "Besides, Gaston is the real detective with remarkable instincts to ferret out guilty thieves and killers. He's almost psychic in his ability to solve crimes. And he works for dog treats."

Robert gave the sleeping pooch a doubtful stare, then spoke quickly, "That's what Vicki's mother told me. She read about you in the *Crawford Daily Gazette*. Told me how you and the dog unraveled several difficult cases, like the murder of the bookstore owner and the pickleball player. You're the only ones who can help me."

"But I don't see how we can help. Your fiancé died from an anaphylactic reaction. It was a tragedy for such a talented woman to die. Her whole life was still ahead. But the matter seems pretty straightforward."

Robert rose to his feet, his voice cracking with emotion, "The police said the same thing. Anaphylaxis, the medical examiner said. They've closed the case. The ruling was accidental death. The police detective refuses to investigate further. The big gorilla told me how sorry he was and escorted me out of the police station. But I believe Victoria was murdered. Someone stole her purse with the epi pen. Deliberately set the bees on her. She would never be so careless." The young man's plea ended on a pitiful note. "I'm begging you. Please help! *Please!*"

Gaston's eyes jerked open. He blinked, then peered at the man for a moment. Suddenly, the pooch scrambled to his feet and jumped to the floor. His high-pitched yelp echoed the man's pleading. After running several times in circles between Sandra and Robert, he plunked down at her feet and gave her a doggy grin.

"There's your answer." Sandra stroked the dog's curly head. "We'll do it!"

Robert opened a small backpack he'd dropped beside his

feet and extracted a gallon zip lock bag with a small olive green purse with silver hardware. Even from where she was sitting, Sandra could see the quality leather craftsmanship of the handbag, and the sturdiness of both the handles and the thin, belted crossbody strap. As he handed the evidence package to her, she saw the small silver edged triangle with the Prada emblem. A fifteen-hundred-dollar purse for sure.

"This is the bag that was left behind. No epi pen," Robert said. "It will have her fingerprints and the theater manager's and possibly the killer's. I begged that detective to run some tests on it and he disregarded the idea. 'Not necessary,' he said. 'A clear-cut case of an accidental death due to a severe allergic reaction.'"

A few strands of hair fell into his teary eyes as he snuffled. "He didn't believe me."

Sandra took the bag from him with the same amount of reverence that she would use if handling the Shroud of Turin. "I'll wear surgical gloves when I touch it. I promise to keep any evidence intact."

He handed her another clear bag with a letter inside of it. "This is the letter Vicki received with the ticket. She threw out the envelope it came in, unfortunately. I tried to contact the editor that supposedly sent it, but I couldn't get past the receptionist. That's why I need your expertise."

Sandra stared at the two zip lock bags probably containing more clues than the gang ever had at the beginning of an investigation. Her eyes gleamed at the thought of unraveling the mystery. "My associates and I will get right on the case. You have my assurance. We'll leave no stone unturned to obtain justice for Victoria."

The young man grasped her free hand with both hands and held it for a heartbeat before shaking it. "Thank you so much. I'm so glad someone finally believes me."

chapter seven

Hail, Hail, the Gang's All Here

"We've got a case, an actual case!" Sandra enthused to Norm Clodfelder, her handyman and partner in sleuthing, as he was kneeling down to fix her ancient snow blower. "Fixing it before the snow flies," he'd told her that morning. Pieces of rusty parts lay scattered on the driveway.

"A client is offering to pay us real money for our detective work. Gaston is finally getting the recognition he deserves. And look! Clues!" She waved the two zip lock bags wildly over his head, nearly knocking off his dingy Green Bay Packer cap.

Norm dropped the wrench he was using to fix the broken machine and rose creakily from his knees. He wiped his greasy hands on even greasier blue jeans and squinted at the two bags. "Whacha got there? Clues? What about a case?"

"You remember last Sunday when Erin found the dead woman at the movie theater?" Sandra prompted.

"The one that died from the bee stings?' Norm scrunched up his face at the mental effort "Freaked poor Erin out. Even Vlad looked pretty queasy when he told us about it."

Sandra nodded energetically. "The victim's fiancé asked to meet with me. He said his partner, Victoria, had been murdered. She was so allergic to bees that she always had her epi pen nearby. He claims somebody stole her purse and set the bees up intentionally, but the police don't believe him. The fat detective in charge threw him out."

"That's a stinging rebuke! I can guess who the bee-ligerant cop is. Our pal, Detective Johnson."

"This man, Robert Doering, wants us to take the case. He heard about Gaston and begged me to help."

"Ya want me to get a flashlight so we can shed some light on the investigation?" Norm gestured toward his crowded workbench in the garage. "I'll bring a mirror to the crime so ya can reflect on the evidence."

Sandra rolled her eyes heavenward. "Seriously, this young man is desperate. He's new in town and has no one else to turn to. I said we'd do it."

"What are ya thinking of charging him? In one of my whodunits the PI charged one hundred bucks per hour plus expenses."

"He doesn't have that kind of money. Besides there's five of us counting Gaston. A hundred dollars even split four ways isn't much. We'll do it gratis."

Norm paused, scratching his chin, before he spoke. "We better call the doc and Beezy. We'll need all the brain power we can get."

***

Vlad and Beatrice arrived at Sandra's immediately after the afternoon classes ended. Dressed in a cinnamon tailored pants suit with a splashy orange hued scarf, Beatrice looked more like a talk show host than a head librarian at the University. She fluffed the top of her short pixie hair. Vlad, thinning hair combed strategically to the side, wore his customary shabby brown tweed jacket with the elbow patches; together they resembled a sparrow and a goldfinch.

Gaston yipped a greeting then trotted into the kitchen. Sandra flitted between the two lovers, scarcely able to contain her excitement. "Gaston and I have been waiting for you all afternoon with Norm. I have some big news. We're officially private detectives!" Her hands fluttered like autumn leaves on a breezy day.

"What's going on?" Vlad turned to Sandra. "You were rather cryptic over the phone when you said we had a new case."

"You told me you had an important visitor. Some man named Robert Doering." Beatrice added. "I never heard of him."

"I didn't want to scare you off before hearing me out." Sandra said. 'It involves the dead woman Erin found at the Classic Cinema, Victoria Fitzgerald."

Vlad tugged on his mustache at the mention of the victim's name, starting to protest, "I don't think we want to..." Beatrice gave him a warning look, and gently patted his arm. His mouth snapped shut.

"I think we should hear what Sandra has to say," she said.

Norm, wearing surgical gloves, was already seated at the dinette table on a red vinyl chair. His fingers folded together formed a tent on the tabletop. He stared at an expensive looking purse in front of him with a puzzled expression. "Hi, Beezy, Doc. We started without ya." He swept a gloved hand over the tumble of objects scattered on the table. "We got a buncha clues. I can't make head nor tails outta them."

Sandra related the events of the morning, ending with the statement, "I told Robert we would take the case. He gave me her purse and the letter from the newspaper editor."

'We don't even know she was murdered. It could have been a careless mistake on Victoria's part that ended in tragedy." Vlad looked skeptical.

"That's what the cop said. From Robert's description it was our old nemesis, Detective Johnson. Don't you want a second chance to prove we are just as good at solving crimes as he is?" Sandra pleaded. "This time we even have clues. Look at the what was in her purse." Sandra pointed at the collection of objects. "Surely there is something in all these items to jump start our investigation."

Chapter Eight
The Case Begins

The four friends stared at the collection of objects before them.

Lipstick. A small bottle of hand lotion. A tortoise shell comb. A handwoven coin purse. A few credit cards and a driver's license in the side pockets. A shopping list. Several crumpled receipts from restaurants. Antacid tablets. A purse-sized notepad with the title of the movie on the first page. Two pens, one with a stylus. Three twenty-dollar bills. A set of keys. A tiny blue metal pillbox.

"What did you say before about motive in our other investigations?" Beatrice asked Vlad. "Your perspective was crucial to solving who put the poison in the pie in the county fair judging case."

"We have to figure out the motive. Revenge. Greed. Love gone wrong." Vlad paced around the kitchen table as he spoke. Gaston trotted along beside him, occasionally fixing curious puppy eyes on Vlad's face as he talked. "All powerful grounds for murder. If the *how* is setting up a deadly allergic reaction, the *why* is even more important. It connects the investigation to the *who*."

"The suspect must have hated Victoria very much to murder her, especially in a movie theater with several people around." Beatrice looked from person to person. "A pretty daring move. The killer took a big chance at being noticed."

"So we're looking for someone fearless. Like one of those guys that go over Niagara Falls in a barrel," Norm tapped two fingers on the table in a staccato beat. "Or those Russian secret agents that slip radioactive poison in the victim's tea."

"Who were those people in the theater? Erin saw four other people there." Vlad stopped to smooth his mustache. Gaston plopped on his haunches, tilting his head to watch. "We have to find out who they were."

"Don't forget the people who worked that night. We can't

rule out anyone except Erin." Beatrice sat down across from Norm. "They all have plenty of opportunity."

"I need to talk to Erin again," Sandra said. "Find out what she knows about the people that were on the Sunday afternoon shift."

Vlad's eyes widened with alarm. "I'm not sure I want Erin involved in this."

"She's already involved. It's better if she confronts her fears instead of burying them." Sandra gave Vlad a pointed look. "Don't underestimate her. She noticed something weird about the bee right away."

"I showed it to my colleague, Mike, who teaches biology." Vlad stared back at her. "He has a friend who is a beekeeper. I've got an appointment to meet with him next week. He's eager to take a look at the strange bee."

"Robert said Victoria received a letter with a matinee ticket from the Arts and Culture editor with the Milwaukee paper. It's in this plastic bag." Sandra held up the zip lock with the letter.

Beatrice struggled into the latex gloves. "Let me handle that part of the investigation. I'll go online and find out if he's legit." She took out the letter and read the name. "Timothy McFarland supposedly sent the letter. It's on the Journal letterhead, but that's easy enough to fake. I'll do some digging on this." She set the letter down on the table.

"What about the junk here on the table? We should take a look at what Victoria had with her." Norm started at the flotsam. "Do all women carry this much junk?"

"Robert swore she left the house with an epi-pen, but there's no sign of it here." Sandra waved her hand over the collection of items on the table.

"Put your gloves on, Vlad. Let's begin," Beatrice suggested.

Vlad picked up the teal cell phone first, studying the window. "This should be helpful. Did Robert tell you the pass code?"

"No, dearie. I'm afraid he didn't," Sandra sighed.

When Vlad pressed the button on the side, the phone remained dark. "It's dead. It's an Apple. Do you have a charger?" He turned to Sandra.

"No, sorry. I have an Android. It was cheaper."

"I have one upstairs, but mine is an older model. I'm not sure the cords are interchangeable." Vlad examined the charging port. "We may have to call Robert to get the right cord."

Beatrice was smoothing out the restaurant receipts. "Victoria seemed to favor Elliot's Inn for lunch. Most of the receipts are from there. One of us should talk to the wait staff. See if they noticed anyone with her. Or anything unusual about her behavior."

"I'm free for lunch tomorrow," Sandra said. "I'll make some inquiries. I haven't been to Elliot's since the place underwent new ownership."

Gaston barked when he heard the word lunch.

"No fancy lunch for you. Sorry, pal," Norm said.

Vlad warned, "You'll need a picture of her to show around. You can use her driver's license, if necessary."

"Wait! There's a phone number on the back of this receipt. It's a 262 exchange. That's the Milwaukee suburban area code." Beatrice's face glowed with excitement. "Maybe it's the elusive editor. I'll track it down. Since I'm already looking at the newspaper staff."

Gaston hopped on Norm's lap and settled down, tucking his head between his paws, but followed the conversation with his eyes.

Norm picked up the pen with the stylus and read the company name emblazoned there. "Fitzgerald's Fine Office Furniture. Shouldn't one of us check out Victoria's family business? After all, she came home to work there. Maybe she ruffled a few feathers being the boss's daughter?"

Sandra snapped her fingers. "Excellent point! Vlad and Beatrice both have offices. Doesn't one of them need a little update?" She arched an eyebrow at Vlad.

He shook his head. "You obviously have no clue how a college operates. No professor or librarian gets a custom-made desk. Too expensive. We get left overs from past instructors. If we're lucky, Purchasing finds an office supply place going out of business and we get a liquidated desk."

"I got a buddy who supplies snacks to all the major businesses in town. I'm sure he has Fitzgerald's as a customer. I can make a delivery there and do a little undercover work." Norm volunteered.

Gaston gave a few loud barks directed at Vlad.

"All right, dog. I hear you," Vlad said with a hint of resignation in his voice. "I'll work on the phone. Sandra, can you contact Robert and get the passcode and the charger?"

"I'm on it. He texted his phone number. I'll text him back."

Gaston sat up, put his front paws on the table, and uttered a sharp yip. Norm patted his head and spoke. "The investigation begins with the Gaston squeal of approval."

Chapter Nine
Supper Club Snoop

Elliot's Inn was a traditional Wisconsin supper club located in the heart of Crawford's downtown. The fake, half-timber façade on top of a brick first floor could have been transplanted from Bavaria, especially with the wrought iron window balcony and steep tiled roof. The building reminded Sandra of the romantic Rhine River cruise, her first experience with crime solving. She carried clippings in her purse from the Amsterdam and British newspapers, extolling the exploits of Gaston in bringing down the ring of jewel thieves aboard the cruise ship.

As she ambled inside the restaurant, her eyes took a moment to adjust to the dim lighting. The overhead fixture created from several stag antlers wired together resembled a bundle of tumbleweed more than a rustic chandelier and cast very little light. Sandra loved the ambiance of the place, viewing the bulky wooden tables and carved chairs through a filmy haze. She half expected a troll to pop out from behind the dark wood bar, as in a Grimm's Fairy Tale. She had to hand it to Victoria, if she were planning something nefarious, this was the perfect setting.

A bleached blonde hostess, hair wound into two doughnuts on each side of her head, bulged through the lacing of her red dirndl. An extremely low-cut blouse with puffy sleeves showed a full cleavage. The wide gathered skirt covered an equally ample derriere. "May I help you?" the woman asked in icy tones.

"I don't have a reservation. Is there an open table?"

The hostess frowned so deeply ridges appeared in her forehead. Her voice dripped with disdain. "There are several open tables, since we have become a *lunch* club in addition to a supper club." She scooped up a menu from behind her stand. "Follow me."

The hostess plowed ahead, leading Sandra into the dining room. A huge fireplace dominated one wall. Its mantel held colorful Bavarian beer steins depicting lush forests, sparkling rivers, and robust ladies in dirndls that fit. Paintings of idyllic landscapes and smiling children adorned the walls. Sturdy oversized tables dominated the center, but Sandra asked for one of the booths that lined two of the sides. She slid into its secluded depths and studied the menu, which featured hamburgers, sausages, and schnitzels, with ubiquitous red cabbage.

A young man in a ponytail wearing fake suede lederhosen appeared at Sandra's booth. Although his black Hoka shoes looked extremely comfortable, the trendy athletic wear clashed with the tall socks and traditional garb. The waiter seemed nonplussed by all the ethnic trappings as he glibly said, "May I bring you something from the bar? We have a nice Riesling as our house wine."

"That would be lovely. May I have a glass of water, too?"

Since there were few diners, he returned promptly with her wine, properly chilled and delicious. She took a slow sip, as the waiter stood poised, pen in hand, to take her order.

"I'm not very hungry," Sandra said. "Can you suggest something lighter?"

"Perhaps you'd like a cup of our oxtail or beer cheese soup? We have a cabbage salad with a caraway dressing," he suggested. "We still have a supper club mentality, including a Lazy Susan that features creamed herring, liverwurst, and the cabbage salad, But that's only available after five."

"I'll have to return some evening and give it a try. Do you work nights, too?"

"Sometimes, if one of the waitresses calls in sick. Mostly I work days."

"My great niece used to frequent this place. Perhaps you know her." Sandra pulled out a picture of Victoria, which Robert had dropped off a few hours earlier, and handed it to him.

The young man studied it. His patronizing expression turned to sorrow as he recognized Victoria. "Yes, she was a regular customer. A very good tipper. Victoria Fitzgerald. I heard about her death. It was terrible!"

"The whole family is in shock," Sandra pulled a lacy handkerchief out of her purse and dabbed at her eyes. "So sad. Vicky was something of a loner. I was wondering if she ever came in with anyone else?"

"No. Usually she was alone." The waiter handed the photograph back to her. "A few times she came in with some guy. I think it was her fiancé. She always flashed around her engagement ring. They did a lot of hand holding and face touching. A long kiss when they stood up."

"That sounds like Robert. Was he tall, thin, with carrot colored hair? Dressed like a prep student?"

"Yeah, That's him. He seemed nice enough. Although she usually paid for the meal."

"Is there anything else you remember?" Sandra tucked the photo and hanky back into her purse."

The young man's face brightened as he nodded vigorously. "The last time she was here she met a woman for lunch. A classy babe, dark hair, in a fancy black dress—long, with a slit up the side. Lots of gold jewelry. Looked real to me. Plus a diamond bracelet that nearly blinded me. Kinda distracted me from her legs. They sat in the booth in the back corner. She drank Manhattans at noon."

"Did you happen to overhear what they talked about?"

"Not really. But it ended with both of them raising their voices. Definitely an argument."

"Are you sure you didn't catch a piece of their conversation?"

"Victoria said she was going to tell everyone about the woman's dirty little secret. Then the foxy lady told her, "You'll be sorry if you do." And she stormed off. Victoria was so angry—didn't even finish her drink."

"You didn't hear what the secret was?" Sandra lifted a quizzical eyebrow. "Vicky liked to play things close to her chest."

"Nope. I didn't pay attention until the yelling started."

"Anything else you recall? Anything out of the ordinary?"

"When she left that day, Victoria gave me a ticket to a movie, a matinee, *Moon Rise Over the Moors*. Said it was an extra. She knew I was a movie buff." He sighed.

Sandra matched his sigh. "She was such a generous girl."

"I saw her at the theater on that Sunday. Alone." The waiter narrowed his eyes. "She didn't even smile at me or say hi, like she didn't want to know me. I figured maybe she was embarrassed about the cat fight."

The hostess sashayed in with three ladies and ushered them to a nearby table. As she handed them some menus, she gave the waiter a gargoyle frown and shot snake eyes at him.

"I better take your order," he said nervously. "My boss doesn't like it if I stay too long at a table."

"I'll have the beer cheese soup," Sandra said. "Does it come with a roll?"

"Poppyseed or rye?" he asked.

"Poppy seed, please. And that glass of water."

As the waiter hurried away, Sandra took another sip of her wine. *So Victoria met with a woman and they argued about a secret. Obviously, the woman didn't want it to get out, whatever it was. Keeping secrets is like sailing a ship over an unfamiliar reef. You never know what rocks lurk beneath the calm surface.*

Chapter Ten
Furniture Factory Foray

Norm nervously jangled the ring of keys in his trousers' pocket. His pal, George, gave him a quick lesson on stocking the soda machine. "Should be no problems with the vending machine today. Sometimes the bottles get stuck and it takes a while to unjam it. Just refill the soda machine and the five shelves of cookies, candy bars, and chips. The biggest job is handling the dolly with all the bottles. Try to tilt it at a forty-five degree angle and move slow."

George was pretty pumped when Norm told him about the case. "I can't believe you're in the detective business, Bro. Sure beats changing oil at the Quickie Lube."

He even lent him a crisp white cap with a Mr. Snack's logo and the matching white polo shirt with fancy Mr. Snack's in curlicue letters appliqued on the pocket. "Take good care of it," George warned. "It's my only spare. My boss gets pissed if we show up in a grungy shirt." Black trousers courtesy of St. Vinnie's completed Norm's disguise. He even polished up his motorcycle boots to look more business-like.

Still, when the grey-haired receptionist peered over the top of her reading glasses to take his measure, he felt like a cockroach who had accidentally wandered onto the queen's tea tray. "What are you doing here? Where's George?" she said haughtily, her eyes traveling down from the top of his cap to the soles of his boots. She wrinkled her nose when she saw the lopsided hem on the trousers, even though Sandra had done her best to alter them to fit.

"He had a family emergency to tend to." Norm answered. He pulled the key ring out of his pocket. "I'm just helping him out." He dangled the keys in front of her and gave her his toothiest smile. "He asked me to sub for him, because he knows I always go the extra mile at work. But then the boss finds me and brings me back."

As he was speaking, a pretty woman wearing jeans and a

yellow Fitzgerald's Fine Office Furniture shirt entered the office from a door marked "Employees Only." She carried a clipboard with a blueprint of an office system of bookshelves and a corner desk unit. A bright blue and yellow, flowered, triangle scarf covered her hair, but a few wispy auburn strands managed to escape and soften the lines on her face. She snickered at his joke, but a baleful glare from the receptionist quieted her in an instant. When the older woman turned her back, the yellow scarf lady winked with one of her sparkling blue eyes.

The receptionist gave him a cold stare and pointed to the door behind the woman. "The canteen is through there. Turn left and you'll see the restrooms on either side of the back wall. The breakroom is between them."

She pushed the reading glasses back on her nose and turned to her computer. Her typing signaled the conversation was at an end. The clipboard woman gave him a sympathetic shrug and cleared her throat, attempting to draw the older woman's attention to the project at hand.

Norm refused to give up. "You know why your computer is cold? Because you left a window open." He smiled at the sullen woman once more.

The woman never looked up, only tapped the keyboard faster. Her forehead scrunched up as her eyebrows drew together in a crooked line. The frown lines around her mouth seemed carved in stone. Norm thought her face would shatter if she smiled.

He pivoted and left the office. Back at the van, he piled cases of plastic soda and juice bottles on a dolly and wheeled it back through the front doors and office. The bottles were a lot heavier and more cumbersome than he had anticipated and needed balancing to avoid tipping. Fortunately the outside door swung inward. He held it open with his hip, as he maneuvered the dolly carefully inside, sticking one hand out to steady the cases of bottles as he pushed with the other. The flower scarf woman was handing the receptionist some plans as he passed back through the office. This time she gave him a fleeting smile, as she pointed to some lines on the drawing placed next to the computer. The grey-haired woman barely glanced up as she dismissed her with a wave of her hand.

Norm was struggling with the door to the floor, beads of

sweat forming under the white cap, when the younger woman kindly held it open for him. "Thank you," he said, wheeling the dolly into the factory much more smoothly with her assistance.

"I'm heading to the breakroom. I can hold that door open for you too." The flowered scarf woman led the way.

The scent of wood stain and varnish overpowered Norm's senses. Several workers were carefully staining a hutch, some filing cabinets and an impressive desk that Paul Bunyan could have used to keep track of logging orders. He kept his eyes moving, watching for obstacles that could trip him up. There were no pieces of wood lying on the immaculate floor, still Norm fixed his eyes on the woman before him. The back of her head revealed a tumble of hair that fell over her shoulders where the scarf ended. She veered to the right to avoid a man wheeling in a mission-style desk chair. Finally she stopped in front of an unmarked door between the ones labeled "men" and "women."

"Here we are," she said and once more, held the door for him.

Norm paused to survey the room. It was a pretty standard break room with a stainless-steel refrigerator, a long granite-like counter containing a microwave and a coffee maker, and solid panel oak cabinets above and below. Light flooded in through the windows lining the opposite wall. The beverage machine and wall to ceiling snack shelves were on his left; two long tables with padded chairs took up the middle of the deserted room.

"My name is Cathy, by the way," the woman said. Her smile lit up her face and Norm couldn't help but smile back. She poured herself a cup of coffee and sat down.

"I'm Norm. I'm helping out my buddy, George." He pushed the dolly over to the beverage machine and unlocked the door. It swung open and he began sliding the bottles into the slots. "Walking through this place reminds me of one of my friends. It was so sad. He drowned in a vat of varnish. He had a terrible end but a beautiful finish."

Cathy laughed. "You have to excuse Mrs. Whelan. She doesn't have a sense of humor. We're all waiting for her to retire, but she doesn't want to give it up. She was here when Fred

Fitzgerald Senior started the company. Then he died and she kept Fred Junior in line. Now that Victoria has passed away, we'll probably never get rid of her."

"I heard about her dying in a movie theater. Stung by bees with a deadly allergic reaction." Norm stopped restocking the soda and sat down across from her. "I had a cousin who almost died from a peanut allergy. If he had even a small amount of peanuts in a cookie, he could kick the bucket. Had to be awfully careful what he ate."

"Yeah, that's what none of us workers understand. Everyone knew Victoria had this allergy. She was so careful, like your cousin. She never went more than two feet away from her epi-pen." Her blue eyes clouded with concern. "Her father was already not in the best of health. Her death has put him over the edge emotionally. In fact, we're all barely keeping it together."

"Is there another employee with enough experience to take over temporarily?"

Cathy looked away as she considered his question. The she lowered her voice to a confidential tone. "I don't want to sound like a gossip monger, but Larry Treptow was in line for a promotion to vice president until Victoria came on the scene. I heard he was a little P.O.ed when he got passed over. Actually, a lot P.O.ed."

"Larry Treptow, huh? Older guy with lots of experience?"

"No. he was in Victoria's high school class. Even dated her for a few months their senior year. Then she went to Columbia in New York for journalism and he stayed in Wisconsin and enrolled at Whitewater for business. They drifted apart. Larry married Sylvia Brandt, the second richest girl in town, after he graduated. End of story."

Two chattering women pushed open the door. When they observed the open door of the soda machine, they stopped talking and surveyed the break room. They spied Norm in his white shirt and Mr. Snack's hat. One of them said, "Are you nearly finished filling the machine? I need my dose of caffeine. Gotta do the Dew!" She jabbed her friend with an elbow and did a little jig.

Norm jumped to his feet and resumed loading the bottles. "Sorry. When I saw this pretty lady drinking coffee, I told her about a pal of mine who died in a coffee factory accident. Fell into a vat of hot coffee."

The two women clucked sympathetically. "How terrible!" the second one said.

Norm gave Cathy a wink as he said, "Not to worry. He didn't suffer. It was instant."

Chapter Eleven
Notes on the Noir

Sandra kept staring at the oversized digital clock as she drummed her fingers on the kitchen table in an erratic beat. The red numbers seemed to light up in slow motion. Each minute marched by like drunken soldiers on a night out. "Where is Norm?" she said aloud. "He should be finished at the furniture factory by now."

Gaston barked and pointed his nose toward the treat jar on top of the counter, but Sandra didn't pick up on his cue. Her mind was a muddle and she had no one to straighten it out. *Who was the mystery woman at the restaurant? How dirty was the secret Victoria knew? Dirty enough for blackmail? For murder?*

Gaston barked again, louder.

"You're right, Lovey Puppy. Sitting here is getting us nowhere. We need to take some action."

"Some action" consisted of slow pacing around the living room with Gaston yipping at her heels. Her Lazy Girl chair looked so inviting. It would be so easy to sink down into it and put her feet up. She seemed to recall sitting with your feet elevated was good for thinking. More blood circulated to the brain. Sandra was about to test that theory out when Gaston hopped on the chair and hunkered down.

Sandra reached to shove him aside when her eyes lit on the *Private Detective Handbook—Large Print Edition* resting on the end table next to the chair. The subheading leapt out: *Discover how the pros uncover facts and get to the truth.* "My handbook was a big help with the last case," she said to the pooch. "Maybe there's some good advice for this one."

When Sandra eased into the recliner, Gaston shifted his position to give her some room to sit. She pressed the controls, the footrest rose, and the toy poodle scooted down and curled up next to her legs. Soon he was snoozing with only a few snorts. Sandra opened the book to the Table of Contents. The weight of the handbook made her wrist ache to hold it upright. If only it had come in a paperback version!

Flipping to the chapter on "Interview and Interrogation Techniques," Sandra found herself reading the section on "Preinterview Preparations" which involved studying attorney's and insurance company's files. None of the advice seemed to fit this case. The only file she had in her possession pertained to grooming her fingernails. Lazy Girl tempted her by whispering, "I'm your best friend, Sandra. We go way back." So she poked at the controls and moved the headrest back. The invitation to rest her eyes for just a few seconds was irresistible. Combined with the glass of Riesling at lunch, she was soon delightfully dozing in competition with her dog for who had the louder snores. The handbook rested facedown on her lap, interrogation advice forgotten.

***

Gaston launched himself off the footrest at the clangorous sound. The sudden movement startled her awake. The thunderous noise was someone knocking on her door. Sandra attempted to rise but the recliner had her in its clutches. She blinked a few times and opened her eyes to get her bearings.

Loud barking came from the entryway. It took her a few moments to shake off the sleep and call out, "Hold on. I'll be right there." A few pushes on the remote and she was standing.

As she shuffled to the door, she heard Norm's voice. "Let me in. I got the name of a suspect."

"I've got some new information, too. It's a doozy," she said as she flipped the bolt on the front door. Norm rushed in still wearing his white Mr. Snack's cap and shirt. He bent down for Gaston's sloppy greeting, and then patted him on the back. He pulled out a Pork Chomps from his back pocket, tossing it to the pooch. Gaston made a spot-on catch and soon crunched happily at his feet.

"You go first," Norm said.

"I interviewed the waiter at Elliot's. He remembered Victoria very well. She was a regular customer and a good tipper. But catch this… The last time she was in, she met a ritzy lady, dressed to kill."

"Aren't you getting ahead of yourself?" Norm said. "We

haven't solved the case yet."

"Hush! I haven't got to the juicy part. She and this woman got into a big fight. Victoria threatened to tell everyone her dirty little secret, the waiter said."

"That could be a motive for murder. Did he say what the secret was?"

"No, he only overheard the end of the argument. The posh lady left in a huff. Victoria was so upset she didn't finish her meal."

"How are we going to find out who the mystery woman is?"

"We need to reconvene all the gang. Vlad and Beatrice will have some ideas." Sandra picked up her phone. "I'll call and leave them a message to meet here tonight. What about your news?"

"I met a woman who works there, she gave me the lowdown about this guy—Larry Treptow—who thought he was going to get promoted to vice president of the company until Victoria came back. Cathy said Treptow was really pissed off when he got passed over."

"Cathy, huh?" Sandra gave him a sly smile. "You're on a first name basis already. I hope you didn't use one of your terrible pick-up lines, like "if you were homework, I'd do you all the time.'"

"Nah, Cathy is too classy for anything that cheesy. She gave me her phone number without me talking trash. But I did tell her some of my dead friend jokes. But I didn't get to the best one about my sister who works at the upholstery factory. She fell into one of the machines. But don't worry. She's recovered."

Sandra shook her head in resignation. "On that note, I'm calling in the team. You need more help than I can muster."

Chapter Twelve
The Man in the Tan Suit

"You don't have to go back to the movie theater," her mother said. "No one will blame you if you quit, after what you've been through."

Erin pulled back her hair and twisted the scrunchie around her ponytail as she checked out her image in the hall mirror. The dark circles under her eyes from restless nights trying and failing to fall asleep were starting to fade. She dabbed a little extra make up to cover them. A whisk of the brush to put some blush on her cheeks, a swipe of tinted gloss on both lips, and she felt ready to go. She thrust out her chin in a defiant pose and said, "No, Mom, I'm going in to work. Mark and Barb are depending on me. Friday nights are always super busy. Just two people can't handle it. Besides, I'm so over the shock."

The teen grabbed her coat from the hook in the hall, and thrust her arms into the sleeves. She squared her shoulders with an approving glance and turned to where her mother was standing.

Mom's face twisted into a cynical frown as she commented, "I hope your father hasn't filled your head with his detective nonsense." She pursed her lips with a puff of air. "Honestly, ever since he got involved with that crazy old lady and her delinquent dog, he's gone off the deep end himself."

Erin shook her head. "Dad has nothing to do with it. I need the money for my car when I get my license in a few months. Besides, I like working at the Classic Cinema. Mark's a good boss." She held out her hand palm up. "Can I have the keys? I can use the behind the wheel practice."

Her mother shouted over the sound of the TV coming from the next room. "Nicholas, please come here for a minute."

The bespeckled eleven-year-old boy reluctantly plodded into the room. "Yes, Mom?" he pushed his glasses back on his nose and calmly met her gaze.

"You're in charge of your little sister until I get back. I'm running Erin to her job at the theater. I should be back in twenty minutes or so. Then I'll order a pizza for supper."

The little five-year-old girl bounded into the room, curly tangles bobbing as she exclaimed, "Oh boy, pizza! Can we order some cheesy bread too?"

"Yes, if you listen to what Nicholas says. Kaitlyn, don't give him any grief. I'm expecting you to be a big girl."

Kaitlyn flung her arms around her mother's waist, "Can't I come along? I like the theater. I want to see Frozen again." The little girl held on so tightly, Maria couldn't take a step without toppling over.

Maria patted the little girl's head, then gently pushed her away. She knelt down to eye level and gave her a stern look. The child stuck her thumb in her mouth as she solemnly returned her mother's stare. "No, Kaitlyn. Erin's going to drive and only one adult can be in the car with her. No one else. I'll be back very soon."

Kaitlyn popped her thumb out of her mouth as she asked, "Can we have ice cream for dessert too?"

"Yes, *if* you're good." She gave both children a brief hug and followed Erin out the door.

"Getting away was easier than I expected," Maria said on the way to the car.

"Getting the car keys was easier, too." Erin grinned at her mother. They rode in silence to the theater, listening to the twang of a country and western song from Maria's favorite radio station.

"Your father will be picking you up at ten," Maria reminded her as she slid into the driver's seat and shut the car door.

***

Erin hung up her coat in the small employees' closet and joined Barb at the concessions counter. The older woman flashed her a smile. "Glad to see you, kid. I was afraid maybe we lost you after what happened last Sunday."

Erin shrugged. "I try not to think about what I saw. I don't want to talk about it."

"I get it. Like Mark says, it's business as usual. The show must go on. Friday night. All the kids will be out to see the new feature. The one about the aliens taking over the minds of scientists. Causing all kinds of chaos, like rockets blowing up, and bombs going off."

The cut-out figure of the handsome young spaceship pilot stood in the middle of the lobby, a welcome distraction from any lingering fears. Soon the elementary school kids and their parents would be in, and any middle school kids who didn't like high school football games on Friday nights. Erin sighed as she remembered bundling up and going to the games with her friends last year, before she decided to buy a car. Kid stuff. She tried not to miss it. Still she felt a pang of regret when her friends gossiped about who was flirting with the cute guys and which football players showed up at Cullen's Dairy without a date.

"Darn this blasted popper!" The greasy basket emitted a cloud of smoke that reeked of burning oil and overdone popcorn. "It's still not working right. Erin, sweetie, can you please get Mark before it sets off the smoke detectors?" Barb was fanning the fumes with a pile of empty bags. The sizzling sound was growing louder and more ominous.

"Where is he?" Erin hustled through the swinging half-door of the concessions area, then ran around the glass candy counter. She paused, uncertain whether to head downstairs to the men's room or across the stand to the labyrinth of upstairs rooms.

"He's in the projection room. Henry called in sick tonight. Mark's setting up the films on the computer there."

Erin swallowed hard before she said in a quivering voice, "The projection room? I've never been to the projection room."

"Go past Mark's office. It's at the end of the hall. You can't miss the lighted room. You'll see the digital equipment and the windows to the three theaters."

Erin froze, reluctant to venture up the dimly lit stairs. She peered uneasily at the threadbare carpeting and the uneven steps. Even though the overhead light was on, some of the bulbs had burned out, causing dark shadows to ooze into unlit corners. She took a tentative step, wincing at the creaking sound of the ancient floorboards. The haze from the popper malfunction drifted into the lobby. Soon the movie patrons would be pouring through the doors. No one would stick around in a smoke-filled theater. She grabbed the handrail and plodded upwards.

Her heart beat faster as she slowly passed the disembodied bare legs of the mannequin. She brushed against a naked foot and it knocked into a stack of old empty reels, sending them clattering to the floor. The noise made her jump with a sharp intake of her breath. She could hear Barb cursing below. Her feet seemed to move forward with a will of their own. Her eyes continually scanned the darkness, looking for any tripping hazards of musty boxes and a broken reel-to-reel projector. A torn life-sized cardboard Chewbacca waved his one intact arm at her as she crept by.

She approached Mark's office and the usual disheveled mess of empty fast-food wrappers and stacks of receipts. The cone shade of the desk lamp cast a spotlight on the ink-stained blotter. The five little windows behind the desk overlooked the big theater. Two metal filing cabinets, drawers hanging open, leaned against a wall. Across the room, a white door propped open by a stack of bricks had a warning: *Keep this door closed at all times!!Customers do not need to hear the platters or the projector!!*

Erin remembered Barb telling her about a little balcony in Mark's office, which used to be the projection room. The five little windows behind his desk were a reminder of its former days. The old projectionist was a Peeping Tom who used the old balcony to spy on the unsuspecting teens making out in the back rows.

Curiosity overcame her good sense. She noticed the black wrought iron railing and crept inside the room, then cautiously stepped past the white door and onto the balcony. As she peered over the edge of the railing, the empty seats below her were shrouded in darkness. It was a long way down.

Leaving Mark's office, she again ventured into the hallway. The teen began to breathe more easily when she saw the bright light beckoning from of the half open door of the new projection room. Safe at last. Erin walked a bit faster.

A rustling noise from behind stopped her dead in her tracks. A cold chill swept over her at the unmistakable sound of footsteps. She slowly turned around half expecting to see the Chewbacca cut-out falling on its face.

Instead a figure in a glowing tan suit glided out from behind the piles of broken equipment. It had no recognizable facial features, just a smear of white, like a mask, under a cream-colored Panama hat. Two black pools for eyes. One bony white hand reached toward her before the thing pivoted away. The wide-lapeled suit jacket flapped eerily as the specter darted into the shadows, and disappeared.

Erin's face drained of all color. Her heart pounded so hard she felt like it punched a hole in her chest. Her breath caught in her throat. She leaned into the wall for support as her knees turned into jelly, no longer holding her erect. A scream escaped from her lips, reverberating through her skull, and throughout the upper floor.

Mark dashed out of the projection room, his glasses askew. He grasped her elbow as she started her slide to the floor. He hauled her to her feet, his face lined with worry.

"What's wrong? Are you hurt?" His eyes filled with concern at the sight of her pale face and trembling body.

Erin pointed a shaking finger directly at the spot where the apparition appeared. "I saw him. He was there. The man in the tan suit. Then he just vanished."

Mark stared in the direction of the torn Chewbacca cut out. "Are you sure you saw a man? Sometimes a draft sets Chewy in motion and I swear I see him moving. But it's just my mind playing tricks on me."

"I know what I saw. It was a creepy looking guy. He stood right over there," Erin insisted.

"The shadows up here can make your imagination work overtime. I'm not denying it can feel a little creepy," he said.

Barb's voice thundered from the bottom of the stairs. "What's going on up there? I need help down here. The popcorn maker is going wacko. If you don't want burnt popcorn, get your butt down here right now."

Mark gave a shrug of apology. "Sorry, kiddo. We'll talk later. We better get a move on before Barb blows a gasket."

chapter Thirteen
Sandra Tooksbury at the Movies

Mark's promise to discuss Erin's sighting of the man in the tan suit was forgotten in the commotion to fix the popcorn machine. A thick layer of sticky grease acted like glue. The lid of the popper was stuck tight, causing the build-up of burnt corn. The fire hazard blew a fuse. By the time Mark went into the basement and reset the fuse, showed Barb how to use some kind of commercial degreaser to remove the oil residue, and dashed back to the projection room, the early bird customers were lining up in the lobby.

"Offer the first comers a buck off the tub of popcorn for having to wait until it's done," Mark said before he climbed the stairs. That was the last Erin saw of him the whole night.

The steady stream of people with their kids kept her and Barb busy, too busy to talk. Even if they had down time, Erin wasn't sure she wanted to tell Barb about the disappearing man. She didn't need another person discounting her sighting as an overactive imagination. It was a relief when the last person for the 9:30 showing of the alien movie straggled into the theater, and Barb stopped filling the popcorn maker.

"Why don't you head home?" the older woman said. "You look wiped out. I can finish up here. I wasn't in school all day."

"Thanks, Barb. I am kinda tired." Erin pulled the scrunchie out, slid it on her wrist like a bracelet and shook her hair loose. Fly-away wisps stuck to her perspiring face. She put on her coat and stuffed her hands into her pockets and slouched toward the lobby doors. The menacing gesture of the skeletal hand reaching for her played again in her memory. She pushed through the lobby doors into the brisk fall night oblivious to her surroundings.

A happy yip startled her out of her reverie.

She knelt down and opened her arms to the poodle. He stood on his hind legs, draped his paws on her shoulders, and slobbered on her chin with puppy kisses as she tried to dodge his drooly tongue. A shabby service dog harness covered his ample torso. With a raised eyebrow, she asked, "Gaston! What are you doing here?"

Sandra answered for him. "We were hoping to have a look around the theater where you found the body. We're investigating the questionable death. The woman's fiancé hired us as private detectives."

Erin stood up as Gaston pranced around her. She saw her dad who gave her a wave from his parked car across the street.

"Your father thought it best if Gaston and I came in on our own. Your boss would easily recognize him. We don't want to arouse any suspicions that would hamper our investigation."

"Tonight might be good." Erin wrinkled her forehead in concentration. "The projectionist didn't show up, so my boss is running the movies. Only Barb, the older lady I work with, is manning the concessions. There's hardly anybody at the late showing."

The flickering neon lights from the overhead display cast strange shadows over the girl's pale face and made the circles under her eyes even darker. Sandra noticed at once. "Is something wrong? You look like you've seen a ghost."

"I think maybe I did." Erin went on to tell her about seeing the eerie man in the tan suit. "Mark didn't believe me when I told him. He said the shadows can play tricks on your mind. But I know what I saw."

"Now Gaston and I definitely need to get inside the movie theater. Do you mind escorting us back in? It won't give you bad dreams to revisit where the woman was murdered?" Sandra flashed her a worried look.

"I'm pretty much over it," she lied, refusing to meet Sandra's gaze. Suddenly she jerked her head up. "Wait! You think she was murdered?"

"Her fiancé does. We're determined to find out the truth." Gaston barked and tugged on the leash toward the brightly lit theater.

"Hold on. Let me check where Barb is." Erin spun around and re-entered the lobby.

Sandra kept a firm hold on Gaston's leash. "Calm down, puppy. Erin will get us when the coast is clear. You know pulling hard on your leash doesn't help my arthritis."

The girl hustled to the concessions area. No Barb. She dashed back to the entrance.

"Barb must be out having a cigarette. Hurry. We can sneak in without her seeing us."

Erin opened the door for the two detectives and led them past the glass cases containing posters of the coming attractions. The sense of urgency was palpable as she tried to hurry them past the counter and the idle popcorn machine. A hint of burnt oil still lingered in the air. The quotes from classic movies almost called out as they walked down the dim hallway. "*A martini shaken, not stirred.*" Sandra couldn't help but read them. "James Bond. *Goldfinger,* "she said. "Sean Connery was the best."

She continued staring at the wall, "*What we got here is a failure to communicate.* O-o-oh. I just loved when Paul Newman said that. They were both so sexy."

"Auntie Sandra, you really have to concentrate. We don't have much time," Erin urged.

The elderly lady stopped before the door with the bold writing: *It's a trap!* and the smaller sentence below: *NO! Really, watch your step.* "What's up with that warning?"

"It's not just a quote from *Star Wars,*" Erin said before she opened the door to the alien movie. "There really is a step down, so you have to be careful." She grabbed Sandra's elbow and gently guided her into the dark theater. Gaston followed meekly behind. "Lovey Puppy, you need to behave."

The elderly woman and the teen were blinded for a moment. As they waited for their eyes to adjust to the dark, Sandra whispered, "How far down was Victoria sitting?"

"Directly in the middle. Middle aisle, middle seat." Erin squinted. A few adults were watching the movie. The families all cleared out at nine.

"Tell me again. How many other people were in the theater and where were they sitting?"

"A couple were down more in the front. A guy with a ponytail was sitting to the left, several rows behind the woman. Another guy—I think—was sitting way in the back, almost to the last row of seats."

"Only four other people. I'm sure the ponytailed man is a waiter at Elliot's. Can you remember anything else about the couple or the guy in the back?"

"Let me think." Erin scrunched up her face. "The couple was kinda bougie, more dressed up than Ponytail. The guy in the back wore a hoodie. A black hoodie with some writing, but he was too far away for me to see what it said."

A man sitting nearby turned to glare at them and hissed, "Shush! Some of us are trying to watch this."

Erin whispered, "Sorry about that," and gestured at Sandra with her finger to her lips in a warning.

Sandra scanned the partially empty seats with a thoughtful look, halting her eyes at each spot that Erin had described. She opened her mouth to ask another question when Gaston wrenched the leash from her grasp and darted toward the last row of seats.

"Damn you, Gaston! I just told you not to tug like that!" Sandra blurted out. Erin scrambled up the aisle to catch him. The pooch yipped excitedly as he ran. She clambered over the thankfully empty seats, muttering, "Gaston. Come here!" The few remaining movie goers craned their necks to see what was going on.

"There's a dog loose in the theater," the shushing man said. "Can't you get him under control? I've half a mind to complain to the manager!"

The dog stopped abruptly and sniffed around the floor. He rose on his hind legs and tugged at something tucked in the armrest of a folded-up seat. A little wooden box was stuck there, but the pooch yanked it free with his teeth. Erin picked up his dangling leash and he led her trotting back to Sandra. Head erect and tail wagging briskly, the box was proudly held high in his mouth.

"Let's go out in the hallway to examine what Gaston found," Sandra whispered.

The two slipped quietly out of the dark room. Erin handed the leash to Sandra and knelt down again by the poodle. He dropped the smoky smelling box in her hand and barked, nose pointed toward the contents of the strange looking contraption. The long rectangular box—about the size of a Pay

Day candy bar, had a fine mesh screen on one side and a circular hole on its narrow end. She stood up and held it to the light of the hallway fixture. She turned it around to get a better look at the contents.

"Oh my God," she gasped.

Inside the box lay a single dead bee.

Chapter Fourteen
No Ghosting Allowed

Eager to share their latest discovery with Vlad, Sandra stepped into the street without looking both ways. Only Gaston's warning bark and backwards tug on his leash pulled her back from an oncoming car. Erin grabbed her elbow again and safely escorted her to Vlad's vehicle, cradling the grungy box in her other hand as though it were a precious Faberge egg. The elderly detective slid in next to Vlad, pulling Gaston onto her lap. "My brilliant psychic pooch found a clue wedged in a seat. Show him the box, Erin."

Erin handed the funny smelling box to her dad as Sandra continued, "That dead bee didn't get into a little box by accident. Whoever brought bees into the cinema did it intentionally. Carried them in this smelly contraption. No killer bees wandered in from the dumpster."

Vlad whistled in amazement as he studied the bee. "We need to compare it to the bee Erin found in her hoodie."

"It's the same kind of bee," Erin said from the back seat. "I know it is. Look at how hairy it is, and the longer antennas. It's just like the bee from the theater."

"From the crime scene, you mean. Some aggressive bees smuggled in by the killer, a missing epi-pen. Her fiancé was right. Victoria was murdered." Gaston yipped as Sandra squeezed him in her excitement. "Sorry, Lovey Puppy. I got carried away."

"When we get to your place, we can make that determination," Vlad said. "I'm assuming you have every clue we've discovered so far in an evidence box."

"Safely stored in a closet in the spare bedroom. I've bagged the restaurant receipts. Our notes on the separate investigations. I'm creating a file, just like my detective handbook says. We can't expect to get paid without documentation of what we've done to solve the case. Speaking of which, have you met with the bee expert?"

"Not yet, but I made an appointment for next week. Now

I'll have two bees to show him," Vlad said as he signaled for a turn onto Erin's street. He knew the street well, since he used to live there until Maria decided their marriage wasn't working for her anymore.

"How about Victoria's phone?" Sandra asked.

"Nothing much." Vlad gave a slight shrug. "Lots of phone calls to her fiancé and friends. A few obvious business calls. Two to the same unknown number that Beatrice is checking."

"Dad, there's more. Something weird happened tonight. The popcorn maker overheated and I went upstairs to get Mark to fix it. It's dark and creepy up there. Mark's got the second floor full of broken junk and cardboard cut-outs from old movies. I was almost to the projection room when I heard a noise behind me. When I turned, I saw a man in a glowing tan suit. He pointed at me, like he was warning me about something, then he vanished. Just like that." She snapped her fingers. "I screamed and Mark came running, but he didn't believe me when I said I saw a spooky man. He said it was probably the flickering light playing tricks on me."

"I know you didn't make up any wild story," Sandra said. "Why would you do that?"

"I'm not the only one. Henry, the projectionist, said he saw the man in the tan suit once. But Barb said Henry was just trying to scare me."

"Are you scared?" Vlad asked. "There's no shame in being frightened. It's a healthy reaction to a dangerous situation. And I should know. I've been in a few of those recently."

"I'm more frustrated than scared. Maybe I was a little terrified at first because I wasn't expecting to see anybody up there. But now I'm just mad because Mark didn't believe me. He was so condescending like I was a ten-year-old kid."

"One of us needs to have a talk with Mark. Something weird is going on in that theater. Would you like me to call him?" Vlad said.

Sandra jumped in. "Let me interview him. I just got some tips from the handbook and I'd like to try them out. Besides, nobody is threatened by a sweet old lady."

***

The cloudless blue sky of Saturday morning made a

mockery of Erin's ghost sighting of the night before. A promise of cooler weather was in the air. The purple coneflowers, which had fat bumblebees buzzing around just days before, were deserted and beginning to lose their brilliant hue, while tiny buds on the mums were starting to appear. Walking with Gaston in the brisk air filled Sandra with newfound energy. She was ready to tackle questioning Mark, gently of course, because the handbook advised to get the interviewee to trust you. How could Mark fail to succumb to her grandmotherly charm and Gaston's toy poodle cuteness?

"Mark always gets to the theater at least an hour before the first matinee," Erin had told her. "He says he likes the quiet before the storm. He unlocks the door because sometimes people come in for gift certificates or to book the theater for a special event. He puts his office hours on the website." The girl reached over the seat and gave Sandra a hug.

***

Sandra left three VM messages, each one basically stating the same request. "My niece insists she saw something unusual last night outside the projection room. You seemed very unwilling to speak to her about it. Erin is a very down-to-earth child and not prone to making things up. Could we please discuss what happened so her parents will feel better about sending her to work at your theater?"

Three times there was no response from Mark. Sandra refused to be ghosted.

"If Mohammed won't come to the mountain, the mountain will come to Mohammed, or to Mark, in this case," she said to Gaston.

Sandra dressed in her nicest little old lady outfit, a lovely woolen knit sweater in powder blue over a flowered print dress. Sensible wide toed pumps and a wide brimmed navy hat sporting a bunch of blue flowers completed the look. She sponged off Gaston's service dog harness to freshen it up before she put him in it. Then she called Norm to pick them up.

"Wow!" he whistled when she walked out to the car. "Are you trying out for the lead in *Driving Miss Daisy*?"

"I never thought I could pull off the old and alluring look, but apparently I'm killing it." She adjusted her hat to a becoming tilt, accenting her red curly bangs and coyly smiled.

"Too bad ya can't tell if the old farts at the Senior Center are giving ya a wolf whistle or if their oxygen tanks just ran out."

Gaston yipped and gave Norm's cheek a big swipe of the tongue, then settled down on Sandra's lap. She rolled her eyes. "You never quit."

The theater doors were open so Sandra cautiously entered the empty lobby. The lights were on but not the heat. "This feels like a morgue," she said to Gaston. "I should have worn my wool coat." She shivered, then wrapped the sweater more tightly around her torso. A faint smell of burned oil was mixed with the scent of pine cleaner. Colorful posters of coming attractions did little to lighten the chill of the atmosphere. There was a display case with photographs of the Classic when it had a round marquee covered with hundreds of light bulbs. A black and white picture showed a slim man with a fedora and a Mark Twain suit standing in front of the ticket booth. In a third photo a long line of people were waiting to see the opening of a movie starring a hometown girl. Sandra felt a wave of nostalgia. Maybe she could have been that girl if she had continued her dance act in Burlesque.

The sound of Gaston's toenails clicking on the bare floor as he scampered around brought her out of her reverie. "We better get down to business, Lovey Puppy." She tightened her grip on his leash as the pair slowly made their way to the concession stand.

"YOOHOO! "Sandra shouted. "Anybody here?"

The only answer was a thundering silence.

A little closet stood nearby with an open door, its single light bulb burned out. A dark green fleece jacket hung inside next to three empty hooks. An ancient industrial vacuum cleaner swallowed up the small space like some forgotten prehistoric beast.

"Mr. Mark," she called again. "It's me, Sandra Tooksbury, Erin's aunt. I called earlier today to talk with you."

Still no answer. She heard footsteps above her head. Gaston barked and looked expectantly at her.

"Oh, darn. I hear you.' She sighed. "We'll have to find the stairs and go up there." The poodle gave a little whine and tugged on the leash. He led her to the staircase across from the concession area. Two bare bulbs dangled overhead.

"At least the steps have lights," she said. She shivered

again, not because of the cold, but because she was remembering her last encounter with stairs—the body she and Gaston found sprawled at the bottom of them. "Let's hope Mark doesn't meet the same fate as Marco. Pushed to his death by a killer."

This time she took the lead moving up the staircase, grabbing the worn handrail for support. The loud creak her foot made on the uneven stairs filled the air. She kept her eyes fixed on the threadbare carpet, not wanting to catch her shoe in one of the rips and go derriere over teakettle back to the bottom. Gaston followed, keeping a step behind. When they reached the top of the stairs, she had to catch her breath before she called again. "Yoo hoo! Anybody here?"

A scuttling sound—probably mice—was all Sandra heard.

Erin was right. The second floor was as creepy as hell. More bare bulbs cast shadows over the wide passageway lined with obsolete movie equipment, and yes, the bare legs and bottom torso of a mannequin that made her think of the wood-chipper in the movie *Fargo*. At least it wasn't covered in blood! The one-armed Chewbacca still stood guard in front of a legion of older life size cut outs. About midway down the hall, a soft light shown from a half open door.

Gaston put his nose to the ground in bloodhound fashion as he led her forward, stopping occasionally and sniffing loudly. The pooch growled at whatever made the scampering noise as it fled into the musty smelling boxes. All the dust made him sneeze so he lifted his head off the floor and studied the boxes and tin reels with his sharp eyes instead. A continuous low growl vibrated from his throat. Sandra didn't know whether to feel cheered that he was keeping watch or alarmed at the ominous noises the dog was making.

She tried calling again, "Mr. Mark, are you there?"

This time a bushy haired man with a salt and pepper beard and black horn-rimmed glasses poked his head out of the lighted room. "Yes, I'm here working in the office. How may I help you?"

Gaston took that comment as an invitation and gave up the search for critters. He bounded into the room, leaving Sandra in the dust. Literally! Then he plunked down before the frowsy fellow and stuck out his paw. The man laughed. "Please to meet you, too, little dude." Then he shook Gaston's paw.

Sandra slowly closed the gap and soon found herself in a room even messier than the office of the gorilla-like police detective. The obstinate cop refused to take Gaston seriously and was quite scornful of their exceptional crime-solving ability. At least this fellow smiled as his eyes rested on Gaston. Another antique projector stood in the corner. The big wooden desk was littered with invoices and half empty Styrofoam coffee cups, while a newer looking laptop and printer took up most of the space. A sign that read "A clean desk is the sign of a cluttered desk drawer" hung on the wall.

Sandra offered the man her hand. "I'm Sandra Tooksbury, Erin's aunt. I left several messages on your voice mail. I'd like to discuss some strange happenings in the theater."

The man looked a bit sheepish as he spoke. "I'm Mark, her boss. I'm sorry. Next week is pay day and all the end of the month bills come due, so I'm a bit swamped here." He gestured at the pile of papers on his desk. Then he lifted an old box of what appeared to be yellowed receipts from the 1950's from a chair and pushed the seat toward her. He settled down on a swiveled office chair that protested his weight with a shrill squeak, and turned to face her. Gaston sat on his haunches resting his head next to Sandra's calf.

"Cute dog. Seems pretty smart," he said. "You said you wanted to discuss something?"

"Erin came home very upset last night. She claims to have seen a ghost, or at least a ghostly looking man. The man in the tan suit, she called him. You didn't believe her, implied it was only her imagination."

"You've seen all the old movie paraphernalia up here, especially the old stand-up figures of actors. Can't you see how an impressionable young girl could be mistaken?"

"Not my niece. She also said another employee had seen the figure earlier in the week. He claimed he was not the only one. Now do you want to call your employees a bunch of liars, or are you going to tell me what's going on?"

Her bright blue eyes shot lasers at him. He squirmed under her relentless gaze until finally he spoke. "There's an old ghost story that been around since the sixties. That's when the long-time manager, Oscar O'Brian, died. Oscar was the manager for forty years, since the heydays of the twenties. Lived in an apartment at the front of the second floor. You walked past its closed door on your way to my office. Chewbacca and a few other old stand ups block the entrance. Nobody lives there now. The owner uses it for storage."

"How does that connect with the man in the tan suit that Erin saw?"

"The projectionist at the time found him dead in his apartment. People claim he loved the Classic Cinema so much that he refused to leave. He always wore a tan suit. I think it's his picture in the display case, but all his contemporaries are dead. There's no one left to identify him in the photo. The theater owner just locked up the apartment, used it to store old equipment."

"So you don't want Erin to talk about what she saw?" Sandra clasped her hands on her lap and waited for him to answer.

"Bad luck always comes in threes. We just had a woman accidentally die in the original theater. I lost an employee two years ago—committed suicide. If word gets out there's a ghost wandering around in the theater, do you think parents are going to want to bring their kids here to see a movie? They'll head down to the mall to the multiplex and pay twice as much to keep their kids safe. People will start saying the Classic is cursed. The multiplex owner would love to see us close our doors."

"I guess you're right. But I should let you know I'm a private detective with a small group of other sleuths. Victoria Fitzgerald's fiancé hired us because he thinks she was murdered. And we found some evidence here last night that supports his contention."

Mark's face grew pale as he stammered, "Evidence? What k-kind of evidence?"

"I can't tell you. It's pretty conclusive. But we need some insurmountable facts to support our case before we involve the police."

Mark dropped his head to his hands as he muttered, "This is even worse than I thought. A murder and a ghost."

Sandra reached over to pat his hand. "Having a few setbacks is a temporary condition. Giving up makes it permanent."

Chapter Fifteen
Beatrice On the Case

When Beatrice stopped for coffee on the way to the library, she picked up a copy of the morning edition of the *Milwaukee Post*. After closing the door to her office so her nemesis and co-worker, Florence Heidt, couldn't spy on her and report any missteps to the Dean, she flipped open the paper to the second page. A small box in the corner had the heading, To Reach the Newsroom, with a phone number for the Arts and Culture section.

A cool professional voice answered on the second ring. "*Milwaukee Post*, Arts and Culture Newsroom. This is Jennifer speaking. How may I be of assistance?"

"May I speak to Timothy McFarland please? It's a matter of some importance." Beatrice tried to make her voice sound just as professional. "It involves a job offer."

"Are you applying for a job? Did you send Mr. McFarland your resume? I can take your name and number and check if you are on the list of applicants to be interviewed."

"No, I'm not applying for a job. It concerns an offer he made to Victoria Fitzgerald. Unfortunately, she's passed away recently. A tragic accident. I found Mr. McFarland's letter among her personal effects, and I'm doing some follow-up work for the family. There's no record of her completing the movie review, as he requested. I'm wondering if she's entitled to a payment for her work. I'm just beginning to make some sense of her estate."

"Are you a lawyer?"

Beatrice crossed her fingers as she lied. "Yes, I am. Her family has asked me to be the executor. That's why I need to speak to Mr. McFarland. There's a lot of unfinished paperwork since her death was so sudden."

"He's on another call right now. Let me transfer you to his voicemail."

After she left her name and number and a brief lie, Beatrice sighed. Several books that she ordered in August had not arrived.

Two of the professors were breathing down her neck because the books were necessary for a student research assignment. School had been in session for a full month and the midterms were approaching.

There was a knock on her door. Before she could even say, "Please come in," Florence, Sour Lady of the Perpetual Frown, poked her head in the door. Her close-set eyes narrowed to black slits when she saw the newspaper spread out on Beatrice's desk. "I'm glad one of us has time to read the paper." Her voice oozed with sarcasm. "The rest of us are trying to straighten out the mess your intern made reshelving books. Don't they teach the Library of Congress system to these students?? If you can tear yourself away from your important work, we could use some help finding the missing books."

Beatrice quickly closed the paper and followed Florence into the stacks. The newly assigned intern refused to meet Beatrice's eyes as she stood red-faced beside an empty cart. The sad looking co-ed nervously pulled on a stray strand of her long hair "I'm sorry,' she muttered. "I printed some wrong labels for the new shipment of nonfiction and put them on the shelves."

Florence sniffed, "When Dr. Provenceno requested the book *Microbiology with Diseases by Body System*, we realized it wasn't where it should be. I pulled the packing list from the last order, so we can begin to track down the books." She waved some sheets of paper in the intern's face.

Detective work would have to wait until the crisis was over. Finding a mislaid book on the shelves was like searching for a gold earring back in a big pile of maple leaves. One by one you had to run your eyes along the row of books until you came to the out-of-order call numbers. Florence grumbled loudly. "How could someone be so stupid?" The poor intern hung her head, her face flushed red. Beatrice saw a tear slide down her cheek. She gave the poor girl a little pat on her back.

By the time Beatrice returned to her office, the voicemail light was blinking on her phone. Of course, she missed the call from the Arts and Culture editor. But he did leave a message.

"This is Tim McFarland speaking. I'm sorry, I'm unable to help you with your inquiry. I don't know anyone named Victoria Fitzgerald. She's not one of our contract workers. I already have a movie critic on staff, so I wouldn't have reached out to any outside reviewers. I hope this is helpful. So sorry for your loss."

A dead end. If the Arts editor of the Milwaukee paper didn't send Victoria the ticket to the Sunday matinee, who did? Probably whoever took her epi-pen and brought in the bees. The murderer was someone who knew Victoria very well. Knew she'd take the bait of writing a movie review for a prestigious paper. Set a trap so her death seemed accidental.

A deep puff of air revealed her frustration. Not only did it take hours to straighten out the stacks, Beatrice had to spend the whole morning working side by side with Florence, who wore her antipathy like a velvet mantle, catching Beatrice in the folds. She missed the opportunity to set up an appointment with Tim McFarland in person. People revealed themselves in body language and facial expressions. Now she had to be satisfied with a disembodied voice on a cell phone.

Her eyes drifted to her purse. There was still the slip of paper with the unknown phone number tucked safely inside a zippered pocket. She stood up and locked her office door. No unexpected visitors this time.

She dialed the number and much to her surprise, a sexy, deep throated voice answered. "Hello, you've reached Voluptas. Desiree speaking. How may I help you?"

Beatrice wanted to say, What the hell is Voluptas? But instead she said, "Please tell me about Voluptas."

"Voluptas Hotel and Spa is the ultimate romantic experience. In fact, we were voted the Best Romantic Getaway In the United States by the International Hospitality Association. We're the perfect couples' retreat with whirlpool suites, massage tables, and a custom designed bed in each room."

"Wow! It sounds just like what my fiancé and I are looking for. Where are you located?"

"We're in Hartland, a quiet suburb northwest of Milwaukee. Would you like me to book a suite for you? It's a paradise of privacy—no windows or telephones to intrude on your romantic getaway."

"I'll have to check with my fiancé and get back to you."

She immediately typed in Voluptas in the computer search engine. The first hit was a Wikipedia entry. In Roman mythology,

Voluptas was the daughter of Cupid and Psyche. She was known as the goddess of sensual pleasure.

That aligned perfectly with the hotel website which featured luxurious rooms, some with giant round beds, flickering fireplaces and small swimming pools in addition to the private spas. "Close to home with flexible times. Stay for an afternoon or several days," the advertisement said. Beatrice called Vlad and filled him in on the dead end with the newspaper editor and her discovery of the getaway hotel. He also looked at the website while they were talking on the phone.

"Wow!" He whistled. "There's no rates listed for the rooms, so it must be expensive. If you have to ask, you can't afford it. Seems like the perfect place for some afternoon delight."

"Did Victoria and her fiancé visit this place or was there something else going on? I think we need to go there and find out." Beatrice clicked on the map with directions. "It's not that far from Crawford. We can be there in forty minutes."

"I'll pick you up after work. See if you can get a picture of Victoria from Sandra. We'll show it to the receptionist. Since we're officially on the case, let's do a little sleuthing."

"I made up a cover story. I'm now a lawyer trying to straighten out Victoria's estate."

Beatrice hung up and immediately phoned Sandra, but her call went right to voice mail. She tried several times but never reached the elderly woman. Most likely she forgot to recharge her phone. Again. No picture of the victim to show the hotel staff.

Then Beatrice remembered. The latest issue of the Crawford University *Alumni News* had a picture of Victoria and her father Fred on the cover, featuring the announcement of her new position of Vice President of Fitzgerald's Fine Office Furniture. She dug through a pile of magazines in her top desk tray until she found the right issue. A radiant blond Victoria with a self-satisfied smirk stood next to a gaunt looking man on the cover. His still handsome face had an arrogant patrician sheen despite the thinning hair and deep circles under his eyes. An expensive suit hung loosely on his broad shoulders.

"Good enough!" she said to herself as she tucked the newsletter into her tote bag and focused her attention back on the missing resource books. The rest of the afternoon was quiet.

Thankfully, Florence made herself scarce and she was able to track down the orders and insist on an expedited delivery.

Vlad picked her up promptly at four. Soon they were driving along the freeway toward Hartland. The directions on her phone were easy to follow, mostly on the major route to Milwaukee, so they made good time until the Hartland exit. Instead of a city street, they entered a one lane, wooded road. A simple white sign with the elegant logo Voluptas underlined with a blue wave greeted them. Gift certificates and tours from one to five p.m. were offered. The winding driveway brought them to a large white two-story building with a cluster of smaller buildings surrounding it.

A gilded double door signaled the entrance. Once inside, a pleasant sandalwood scent permeated the lobby that was tastefully filled with oversize white leather furniture. Nearby sat an enticing, beautiful love seat—the perfect spot for a tryst. Beatrice felt she could sink up to her ankles in the lush carpeting. An exotic looking woman with long black hair wearing a blue silk dress stood behind the marble topped reception desk. Her red and gold name badge read Desiree.

"Welcome to Voluptas. How may I help you?" She smiled as though she shared an intimate secret with them. "Do you have a reservation?" When they didn't immediately answer, she turned to her computer. "If not, we still have a few rooms available on short notice. Not the ones with a pool, unfortunately."

Vlad trailed behind Beatrice. A gauzy painting of two naked nymphs gathered around a well-endowed young man hung over the entrance. The Impressionistic style of the tastefully arranged threesome gave it a dreamlike eroticism. Vlad's eyes grew wide and his breathing came a bit faster as he studied the painting. Walking backwards to fully appreciate the Renoir-like talent of the artist, he stumbled on a small table filled with glossy brochures. His hip caught the table's edge and sent the pile of advertisements flying to the floor. As he bent to hastily scoop them up and stack them as before, Beatrice shot him an annoyed look.

Vlad hurried to catch up. He swept his gaze over the elegant lobby, only resting a few seconds longer at the distracting artwork before he spoke. "This place is amazing. Reminds me of Coleridge's poem, "'In Xanadu did Kubla Khan a stately pleasure dome decree.'"

"That's quite lovely," the woman flashed him a welcoming smile. "You said it was from a poem. Who wrote it?"

"Samuel Coleridge. He's one of the Romantic Poets."

"Can I find him on Spotify?" she asked. "I'd like to hear the whole song."

"Sorry," Beatrice broke in. "He's been dead almost two hundred years. But you can probably google him on the internet and find it."

"Are you interested in a room?" the young woman repeated, batting her fake eyelashes at Vlad,

"Uh, no," he gulped, fixing his gaze upon a spot on the wall behind the reservation desk. "Not this time."

Beatrice inched in front of Vlad. "I'm hoping you can help us with clearing up a legal matter. My client passed away suddenly. We believe she frequented your establishment and hope you can confirm her membership. If so, I am wondering if there is any monetary value of her membership that should be included in her estate."

"Our memberships are usually non-refundable. I'd have to check with my boss. He's not here right now." Desiree looked down at her manicured nails and fluttered her fingers. "He won't be back until tomorrow." She stifled a yawn.

"Oh, dear. We traveled several hours to get to Hartland." Beatrice gave Vlad a little kick to his ankle. He flinched, then gave the receptionist a charming smile.

"Maybe you could help us make sure we've come to the right Voluptas. I noticed there was another establishment in northern Illinois," he said.

"Oh yes, We have one in Kenosha, too." Desiree smiled back. "Corporate is considering opening one near Lake Michigan, as well."

"Could you please look at the deceased's photo and see if you remember her visiting here?" Vlad pleaded. "Miss Krupp, could you show Desiree the photo?"

Beatrice took the picture of the Fitzgerald's out of her bag and laid it in the desk. "Do you recognize this woman?" She pointed to Victoria.

Desiree studied the picture for a moment, then shook her

head, as her long hair swirled becomingly. "I've never seen her before." She pointed one carefully polished finger at Victoria's father and tapped on his picture. "But the gentleman in the photo looks familiar. He's been here several times, always with the same woman. Not the blonde." Her brown eyes grew troubled and her voice dropped. "Oh, no. I shouldn't have said anything. We're supposed to honor the confidentiality of our customers. I can't tell you anything more."

"Are you sure it was him?" Vlad asked kindly.

Desiree smiled flirtatiously and fluttered her fake eyelashes at him. "Positive. I never forget a man's face!"

Chapter Sixteen
Bee-ware the Mighty Sting

"Victoria's father was up to some hanky-panky and Victoria must have found out about it," Vlad said as they pulled away from Voluptas. "But with whom?"

"Do you think it could involve the mystery woman Victoria met at the restaurant?" Beatrice excitedly tapped her cheek. "The waiter heard them arguing about some dirty little secret. Boinking Fred Fitzgerald fits the description of dirty. Both of them would want to keep it secret."

"Victoria may have been doing some detective work of her own. We need to find out who the mystery woman was. What's the connection?" Vlad carefully merged with traffic as they entered the freeway for the journey home.

"And how do the bees fit with all of this? The sexy woman at the restaurant carrying a smelly box of bees into a movie theater doesn't make sense. Although it could fit in her purse like a Snickers bar." Beatrice took out a restaurant receipt and smoothed it out on her lap. "I wish Elliot's had video surveillance so we could check out what the woman looked like. But it's just a small-town restaurant."

"Beezy, You're a genius! Maybe Elliot's doesn't have CCTV but the jewelry store next to the movie theater does. I've noticed their security cameras when I walk by. Maybe we can find out who came out of the movie theater that afternoon! It could be our mystery woman."

"Do you have time to check it out tomorrow?"

"No. Tomorrow I have a date with a beekeeper in the morning. I'm cancelling my office hours. Could you head to Legacy Jewelers when they open?"

"I'm sorry. I have a staff meeting tomorrow. If I miss it, Florence will complain to HR that I'm not performing my duties. She still holds a grudge because I got the promotion to head librarian instead of her."

"We'll have to ask Sandra to check it out. Maybe her private detective handbook has a chapter on surveillance cameras. She can take Gaston with her."

***

The driveway to the beekeeper's place was long and winding. Evergreen trees hid the house from the road. Vlad felt like he was driving down one of Wisconsin's rustic highways, due to the number of trees waving their varicolored limbs in the thin September sunshine. After the last twist in the road, Dave's large clapboard two-story house appeared. A slim man in a full mustache stood in the driveway dressed in a white jump suit and knee-high olive-green rubber boots. He gave a friendly wave and stepped over to greet him once he'd parked the car.

"So you want to learn about bees?" Dave said in a hearty voice as he pumped Vlad's hand vigorously. "I'm about to check up on the honey production, so you're here on the right day. Got lots of beekeeper gear in the garage. We can get started whenever you're ready."

"Actually I was hoping you'd recognize some unusual bees we recently found. They don't look like honey bees or bumble bees. One of them died in a little wooden box. I brought that along, too."

"Bring them into the house and we'll see what you have."

Vlad picked up the smoke-scented box from the passenger seat with one hand. He carefully lifted the plastic bag with the two dead bees nestled on a paper towel with the other and followed his host as he led the way through his garage. They walked past a large stainless-steel cylinder that resembled a giant coffee urn on a tripod. "That's the electric honey extractor. Sorry I can't show you how it works. We're not ready to harvest the honey for a few weeks."

'That's ok. Identifying these bees is the main reason I'm here."

Dave opened the door for Vlad and ushered him through a laundry room into the kitchen.

"Have a chair." Dave sat down at the oversize kitchen table and gestured at the seat next to him.

Vlad laid the box and the bees on the table before the man. "Can you tell me what these are?"

Dave picked up the rectangular box with the mesh screen and turned it around in his hand. "This is a queen bee cage. Only it's a bit larger than the ones I have. See that hole." He pointed to the circular hole drilled into one end." That normally is filled with a sugar plug. We transport the queen to a new hive in this. The worker bees eat the sugar and set her free inside the hive."

"How do you catch a queen bee without getting stung?"

"I've done it several times. You have to be a skilled beekeeper to do it. I grasp the two wings together without putting any pressure in any other body part. Then I put her in the cage a and seal it."

So the killer has to be a skilled beekeeper, Vlad thought. "Can you trap other bees like the ones we found?"

"You can create a bee trap with a flower and honey in a jar. Smear a little honey under the flower—not globs of it—and wait for the bee to be attracted to the sweetness. When it lands on the flower, snap the lid on the jar."

"Can you transfer the bee to the smaller cage then?"

"You could but why would you want to? Seems like a lot of effort for little pay-off unless you're trying to move some problem bees, like carpenter bees."

Vlad thought, *Or trying to murder an allergic woman in a deserted movie theater.* But he said, "Good question. The queen is the real prize, I suppose."

"You got that right." Dave turned his attention to the clear plastic bag. "I can tell right away these are long horned bees. See how hairy they are?"

Vlad nodded. "We noticed when we looked up close that they had longer hair than honey bees."

Dave continued, "The one with the broken antenna is a female and the one with the long antenna is a male. The longer the antenna the more attractive he is to the female."

"Bees aren't the only species where the females are attracted to long male parts," Vlad joked. "How would you lure these two out of a hive?"

The beekeeper shook his head. "Long horned bees don't live in hives. The females are ground nesters—they dig holes in the ground to create burrows for their offspring. Typically they nest under shrubbery. The males hang out together on leaves."

"So how would you find them?" Vlad stared intently at the strange bees.

"Find the males and the females won't be far behind. They aren't as aggressive as honeybees, so catching them would be easier."

"But they still sting?"

"All female bees sting. Their venom can be just as deadly if someone is allergic. Any more questions before we get started with the hives?" Dave stood up and strode toward the garage. "A cool morning is the perfect time to check out the bees. They move slower in colder temperatures."

Vlad picked up the box and the dead bees, and followed him once again. "I don't want to take up any more of your time. I should be going." He moved toward his car. Dave took a bulky white jumpsuit off a hook and held it out to Vlad. "Just set your stuff on my workbench and put this on. One size fits most. You may get a little warm in the heavy cotton and mesh, so take off your jacket."

Vlad placed the evidence in an out of the way spot on the workbench and took off his warm-up jacket. He slowly walked toward the white suit like a death row prisoner on the way to the electric chair.

"Take off your shoes," The beekeeper ordered.

Vlad kicked off his loafers and stepped in the white garb zipping it carefully up to his chin. He noticed the beekeeper's suit had built in feet that flopped about as he took a step.

"Do I walk to the hives without my shoes?"

"No, you'll want to slip them back on." Dave wrinkled his nose at the Vlad's loafers. "Darn, I should have warned you to bring boots or wellies."

Vlad stuffed his feet into the shoes. The extra bulk from the beekeeper's suit made it difficult to get them on. His feet felt pinched and his toes began to cramp. "Do we have far to walk?" he asked.

"Only over that hill," Dave gestured toward a rise after the bend in the driveway. Vlad looked at the distant hill and his newly polished loafers with the white fabric bulging out and sighed.

"Next, put on your hat." The wide-brimmed hat had a mesh veil connected to a circular frame the same size as the hat's brim.

The mesh extended beyond the ring and was then gathered with a bit of elastic. Vlad felt reassured when he saw the elastic on the bottom. Only a seriously pissed off bee would attempt to get through the veil.

"Here are your gloves." Dave handed him a heavy pair of elbow length gloves. Every inch of his head and body was now completely covered and protected, like an astronaut about to take a step on the moon.

"We're set to check out the hives. You're on an exciting adventure! I'm so glad I took up raising honeybees when I retired. They are fascinating little creatures," Dave said cheerfully. The Mr. Rogers of beekeepers picked up the handle of a coaster wagon with a plastic cat litter container now filled with beekeeping tools and marched up the hill with Vlad lingering behind him. "I've had these bees for three years now. I lost the last hives to a mite infection. But these bees seem healthy and happy. They're good producers and very friendly. I've never been stung."

Dave stopped by the first of three hives. It consisted of two white boxes and a green one stacked on top of each other. He pulled a device out of the wagon that looked like an oil can with a bellows attached. After flipping open the lid to reveal a pile of shredded material, he dropped a lit match onto it, then slammed the lid shut. Immediately smoke poured out of the spout. Then he lifted the green box off the hive and aimed the smoking canister at the groups of bees swarming over the wooden frame of the next layer.

"I need to hit the bees with a cloud of smoke to prevent them from producing pheromones. Bees warn each other of intruders by their sense of smell. You'll see a little smoke makes them quite docile, so I can do this." He lifted a wooden slat partly covered with waxy honeycombs. Honey dripped out of some open cells at the bottom. "When this is completely covered with the wax it's time to harvest the honey."

"How much honey do you usually harvest?"

"Last year around two hundred and forty pounds."

Vlad whistled incredulously. "From just three hives? Wow."

"Come a little closer. I'll try to find the queen for you. I can lift this part up. She should be in the next layer."

"No. No. That's alright. I really should be getting back to work." Vlad pivoted around to leave, but his foot got stuck in a slight indentation in the grass. His shoe became wedged in the hole and he stepped out of it. Luckily, he had the protective gear on in case he disturbed any bees on the ground. As he bent down to free his loafer and squeeze his foot back into it, his hat tilted forward blocking his vision. The clumsy gloves made it difficult to grasp the errant shoe and pull it out of the hole. He felt for the loafer with one hand and pushed the flopping hat back with the other. He finally found it.

"Would you like some help with that shoe?"

"No thanks," Vlad said. "I've got it."

As he thrust his foot into the shoe, he lost his balance. His hat was knocked askew; only the elastic kept it on. He thrust his hand out to catch himself from falling but instead bumped the second hive. A cluster of annoyed bees flew out of a little hole on the side and discovered the disturbance. The squadron formed to dive bomb Vlad, but Dave was right there with the smoker. He aimed a cloud of smoke at the honeybees and they dispersed. Vlad got a lungful of smoke and began to cough.

"Are you all, right?" Dave asked.

When Vlad finally stopped coughing, he said, "I'm fine. Thanks for saving me from the bees."

"Aw, they probably wouldn't have hurt you, They're a bunch of little sweethearts. Better to be safe than sorry."

"I'm going to go now. Thanks you for helping me identify the strange bees."

"Glad to be of service," Dave said cheerfully. "Can you find your way back to the car? I really need to check the other hives to see how the honey production is going."

"Yes, I'll be fine. Thanks again, Dave."

Once he cleared the crest of the hill, Vlad took off the floppy hat. Away from the smoke, his lungs began to clear. His eyes were still a little watery, and tears blurred his vision. He blinked several times until the blurriness disappeared. An arm brushing across his face took care of his drippy nose. Slowly he made his way through the trees. Leaves and twigs crunched under his throbbing feet.

An ominous buzz seemed to follow him. Vlad lifted his

gloved hands to press against |his ears, but the buzz must be coming from outside. Suddenly he felt a sharp pain at the back of his head.

"Ouch! That hurts like hell." he cried.

One of the little sweethearts extracted her revenge for his attack on the hive. He could feel the welt forming.

As Vlad watched the honeybee fly erratically away, he remembered a line from Shakespeare. *"Though she be but little, she is fierce."*

Chapter Seventeen
No TV Guide for CCTV

"Of course I'll go to the jewelry store," Sandra said the next morning when Vlad stopped by on his way to work. He told her about his meeting with Dave, the beekeeper, omitting his fall into the second hive and the subsequent smoke rescue.

Sandra got a far-away look in her eyes. "I have some fond memories of shopping with my late husband, Howard. I always told him, 'I have enough jewelry said no woman ever.'"

"You're not shopping. You're going to check out Mr. Bradley's surveillance cameras to see if he has any videos of the people leaving the theater on the Sunday when Victoria died, September 22, at five," Vlad reminded her. "Do you need to write the date and time down?"

"No, dearie. I can remember. I may be old but I never forget the important details when I'm on the case."

"Pat's a good guy. I'm sure he'll help with the investigation if you tell him what we're looking for. When I was shopping for Beatrice's engagement ring, he was very helpful. He even gave me a discount so I could stay within my budget. He's that kind of person."

"I think jewelers get a bad reputation, like lawyers." Sandra looked at the clock. "I suppose I should get going."

"Take your cell phone. Ask Pat to pause the video feed. You can snap a picture of the folks coming out. See if he'll hold on to it, in case we finally convince Detective Johnson Victoria's death was premeditated murder. And take Gaston with you. A dog comes in handy to soften a witness."

"I'll take the clippings from the Daily Gazette to show him all the other cases we solved. Mr. Bradley will know we mean business." Sandra's eyes gleamed at the thought of expounding on the exploits of her crime solving pooch.

An hour later Sandra was waiting by the door in her cropped, faux fur jacket that accentuated the lines of her silky purple jumpsuit. She only wished she could have worn her stilettos, but she had to give them up for more sensible athletic shoes. After their last case, she had come to the conclusion you can't flee from killers in high heels, especially if you're pushing eighty, or more. Jewelers probably didn't pay much attention to customers' feet. Anyway, toe rings weren't a big seller in Crawford. Gaston was in his usual Service Dog harness, but she did put a blingy rhinestone collar around his neck.

Norm whistled when he saw them. "Ya look very high class. What's classy if yer rich but a no-no if yer poor?"

Sandra shook her head as she climbed into the car. "I'll bite."

"Taking money from the government."

She laughed as Gaston hopped on her lap. "I suppose you have a jewelry store joke?"

"Lemme think. This old white haired guy walks into a jewelry store on a Friday night with a beautiful young woman and says to the jeweler, "I'd like to buy a special ring for my girlfriend." The jeweler looks through the display case and pulls out a $5,000 ring. The man says, "No, I want something more special."

"So the jeweler goes to his special stock and brings out a $40,000 ring. The woman's eyes sparkle and she trembles with excitement. The old guy sees this and says, "I'll take it." The jeweler asks how the payment will be made, and the old man says, 'By check. I know you need to make sure my check is good, so I'll write it now and you can call my bank on Monday morning to verify the funds. I'll pick up the ring Monday afternoon.' On Monday morning, the jeweler phones the old guy, mad as hell, and says, 'Sir, there's no money in that account.'

"I know,' says the old man. 'but let me tell you about my weekend.'"

"Sounds like something you'd try," Sandra smirked.

"Nah, I ain't that classy. I wouldn't go shopping at no jewelry store. If I can't get it at Farm and Fleet, it ain't worth getting."

Norm dropped her and Gaston off at the front of the jewelry store. "I'm heading to Swig's for a cuppa coffee and some breakfast," he said. "Call me when yer done." Then he drove off.

The Classic Cinema next door looked abandoned in the daylight, its lobby dark and marquee unlit. Sandra looked up to see a gleaming white security camera mounted on the wall between the two businesses. It had a clear view of Legacy Jewelers' door and display window. and the front of the theater. Her heart beat a little faster at the thought of identifying the movie goers from that day.

"I hope Mr. Bradley keeps the recorded footage for longer than a week," she said to Gaston. "Now we may be getting somewhere in the investigation."

He yipped in reply.

A bell tinkled when Sandra opened the door. A white-haired lady arranging earrings at the rear of the store greeted her with a friendly smile. The handsome grandfather clock in the corner read five after ten. "Please let me know if I can help you with anything."

Sandra's eyes were drawn to the beautiful necklaces in the front display cases. A sapphire pendant lay on a white velvet pad, a large emerald surrounded by tiny diamonds was next to it, a delicate amethyst dangled on a thin gold chain. For a moment, she forgot their mission. The lovely necklaces reminded her of an earlier time shopping arm in arm with Howard for their tenth anniversary. How his eyes shone with pleasure at her happiness when she tried on his gift necklace! She let out a loud sigh.

The woman moved near to them. "Perhaps you'd like to take a closer look at one of the necklaces?"

Sandra gave her head a little shake. *Back to reality.* "No thank you. I'm here to talk to Mr. Bradley."

"Let me get him from the back of the store." The salesclerk disappeared behind a divider at the back of the store. A cheerful bald man with a grey goatee and twinkling brown eyes appeared in her place. "You wanted to see me?"

"Hello, Mr. Bradley. I'm Sandra Tooksbury and this is my dog, Gaston."

Gaston sat down and extended his paw, waving it in the air. Mr. Bradley laughed, and came around the counter to give it a shake. "Cute little fellow. And smart."

"Famous, too," Sandra said. "He's helped solve several crimes. He caught an international jewel thief and two murderers."

The older woman who had returned to boxing pairs of

earrings exclaimed, "I remember reading about him in the newspaper!"

"Wasn't he on TV too?" Mr. Bradley said. "I saw him a couple of years ago on some talk show. He helped capture some terrorist with that professor from the university. You were on the show with them. It was a remarkable story."

"Yes, that was Gaston," Sandra said proudly. "He's known all over the world for his instinct for solving difficult cases. He even got a reward from the university for foiling a bomb threat. Some jewel merchants in Antwerp also rewarded him for recovering some of their stolen gems."

"What are you doing here? Did you hear about our new shipment of diamond rings? Is someone planning to rob my store?" Mr. Bradley's eyes widened in alarm. "I have a new high-def security system with eight cameras. The one outside even has infrared for night vision. I thought I had all bases covered."

The older woman gasped, "Oh, no! I knew the word would get out about that big order."

He locked eyes with her. "You were right. I should have invested in a better safe, too."

"No, no dearie." Sandra patted him on the arm. "It's nothing like that. Just the opposite. We could use your help in solving our latest case."

The man looked visibly relieved. "How can I help?"

"Is there somewhere we can talk in private?"

"Come this way. We can close the door to my office. Alice, please make sure no one disturbs us?"

"Of course, Mr. Bradley. If someone comes in needing your assistance, I'll ask them to come back in an hour."

He ushered her past his workroom where a wood workbench held an assortment of loose gems on a mat. A magnifying light with an adjustable arm shone a spotlight on a ring with a missing stone. Various tools surrounded the ring. Sandra recognized some tweezers but all the others were too high tech for her. Gaston trotted meekly behind her and the jeweler.

The man opened the door to a back office with high quality furniture. The "L" shaped desk was polished to a fine sheen. The imposing hutch had two cabinets separated by an elaborately carved shelf. The curved overhang made the hutch seem larger, as did the raised panel sides and back of the desk. An old fashioned looking safe stood against a wall in contrast to the laptop computer very new in appearance sitting on the desk.

"What a beautiful desk!" Sandra said, as she sat down in the proffered chair. Gaston leapt onto her lap, his bright eyes alert and watchful.

"I had it custom made by Fitzgerald's," said Mr. Bradley as he sank into his leather swivel chair. "It was a bit of a splurge but it was made to last. Heirloom quality. Now I'm sure you're not here to discuss office furniture. Why have you come to see me?"

"A woman died two weeks ago in the theater—anaphylactic shock from a bee sting. She was highly allergic and had no epi pen."

"I read about the accidental death in the paper. Victoria Fitzgerald. Some bees got in when an employee went out for a cigarette and propped open the door. What a senseless tragedy!" His face drooped in a mournful expression. "I know her father well from Kiwanis. Nice fellow."

"Victoria's fiancée believes it was no accident. He saw her leave for the theater that day and swears she had her epi pen, Her purse was found near a trash can; no epi pen. Robert claims she would never leave her purse behind. The epi pen was always within reach. She feared another bee sting meant death."

"It's a damn shame. Fred has been thinking about retiring—health problems, you know. Victoria came home to learn the ropes and take over the business. But what does her death have to do with me?"

"You have a security camera outside your store close to the Classic Cinema. I'm hoping you still have the footage from September 22. We can see who left the matinee that day. One of them might be her killer."

Mr. Bradley fired up the computer. "I invested in state-of-the art digital equipment. The video recorder goes back a whole month. We still have all of September on this." He scrolled through a catalog of dates until he came to correct day. Gaston barked sharply hopping on her lap as Sandra moved her chair close to the storeowner's.

"What time should we be monitoring?" he said peering intently at the screen.

"The show let out about five." Gaston put his paws on the desktop as the footage from that Sunday afternoon came up. The picture was as crisp and clear as if they were watching a movie on Bluetooth. At a few minutes after five, Sandra recognized the waiter from the restaurant as he came onto the screen, hands in his jacket pockets, slouching into the drizzly rain. Next a woman appeared. She flipped the hood of her full-length raincoat up to protect her head, but Sandra caught a glimpse of flowing black hair before she quickly moved out of view. Gaston yipped excitedly. A pale, hatless man followed, the top of his balding head caught the glare of the overhead streetlight. He scanned the street in a few jerky movements before briefly turning his face toward the camera, then he disappeared as well.

"Well, I'll be damned. I know that fellow." Mr. Bradley thumped his fist on the desk and rose to his feet. He rewound the video and paused it on the man's face. His voice cracked with excitement. "I'm positive he's the man who sold me this custom workstation. His name is Larry. Larry Treptow. From Fitzgerald's Fine Furniture."

chapter Eighteen
Drinking 'til We Drop or an Idea Pops

Gaston rocketed frenetically around the living room, nearly knocking a porcelain lamp off the end table. It wobbled back and forth. Norm was sitting next to it and immediately set it right. He tried to distract the dog by waving a stuffed sock monkey at him, but the pooch ignored his favorite toy and continued racing as fast as his little legs could move.

"This is no time to get the zoomies," Sandra scolded. "Beatrice and Vlad will soon be here. We have serious business to discuss."

The little dog only ran faster.

"He's only running in circles because it's too hard to run in squares. Right, Little Buddy?" Norm picked up a rawhide bone and tossed it toward Gaston. "Here's a tasty chew toy." The dog picked up the bone and scurried with it to the credenza. He dropped it behind the sideboard and then picked up the pace around the room.

"Well, that was a wasted effort," Norm said.

"My warning goes for you, too," Sandra said, shaking her head. "We need to put our heads together and think. This is a tough case."

"Not for yer psychic pooch—the Great Houndini. He's just getting warmed up." Norm took a sip of his beer as the pooch zipped by again. "Ain't ya forgetting to mix your special martinis?"

"Oh, dear. That dog has got me so flustered. I need to keep things on track." Sandra hurried over to the liquor cabinet and lined up three Martini glasses on top, then took out her expensive bottle of gin—the one she kept for special occasion—and a bottle of vermouth. She poured the alcohol into a silver shaker and pretended she was playing a giant castanet to the tune of *La Cucaracha.*

They heard a knock at the door. Gaston stopped running in circles and hurried over to the foyer instead. He stood on his hind legs and pawed at the door. His excited yips filled the entryway.

"Could you please get that, dearie? I'm a little busy here," Sandra said between shakes. She added a little shimmy as a finishing touch.

Norm lumbered to the door and swung it open with a hearty 'Hi-ya!' Vlad and Beatrice stepped in and hung their coats on the hall tree. Gaston yipped as he circled around the two sleuths, then dropped at Beatrice's feet, wagging his little tail so hard his whole behind was in motion.

"What a greeting!" Beatrice laughed as she bent down to embrace the quivering dog. She turned her head from side to side as Gaston regaled her with doggy kisses. "I haven't had a welcome like this since I came back from a week-long librarian conference." She looked affectionately at Vlad, and he winked at her. "All that's missing are the candles and wine."

"Martinis will have to do." Sandra poured the contents of the shaker into the glasses and plopped an olive in each. "Come and get a drink. Make yourself comfortable. We're going to figure out what we know so far." Drink in hand, she glided to her recliner and took out a pad and pen from the end table drawer. Gaston left Beatrice to hop on her lap. She absent-mindedly stroked his back with her free hand. All the exercise mellowed him out and he snuggled next to her.

"Let's hear what you've been up to." Norm settled back down on the couch by his beer. He propped his stockinged feet on the coffee table; his pink big toe stuck out from a hole. "Beezy, you go first."

Beatrice stared at the grayish socks then took her place across from him on the love seat while Vlad grabbed two martinis for them. He handed one to her before sitting down at her side, cradling the drink in his hand. She smiled gratefully at him before speaking.

"I contacted the Milwaukee newspaper first, but the arts editor said he never heard of Victoria Fitzgerald. No job offer there. The man never heard of her."

"So the letter was a fake. The ticket was a ploy to get Victoria to the scene of the murder." Sandra tapped the pen on the side of her cheek as she wrinkled her forehead. "I surmised as much. The murderer obviously knew her well enough to appeal to her ego." Then she jotted down a few notes about the false job offer.

"And well enough to steal her epi pen and purse," Vlad added.

"A lot of people knew she had a severe allergy. We have to narrow it down to who had opportunity. Please continue." Sandra gave Beatrice an encouraging smile.

"Then I called the number on the back of the restaurant receipt. Bingo! It's a love nest masquerading as a hotel and spa. Some place called Voluptas. Vlad and I went to visit. I was posing as a lawyer—the executor of Victoria's estate. I showed the receptionist a picture I had from the alumni news of Victoria and her father. She didn't recognize the victim, but she sure zeroed in on her father. He'd been there several times with a young woman."

Norm whistled. "So her father was having a booty call with some babe."

"Then the receptionist clammed up and said she'd get in trouble if she talked anymore." Beatrice shrugged. "That's as far as I got."

Sandra's eyes widened as she snapped her fingers. "The waiter at Elliot's told me that Victoria got into an argument with some ritzy mystery woman and threatened to tell everyone her dirty little secret." She wrote mystery woman in caps with a big question mark.

"A dirty little secret, huh? Wonder what that could be…" Norm said.

"Another mystery woman. Could they be the same person?" Vlad wondered aloud. "Whoever it is, they have to know something about bees. When I visited Dave, the beekeeper, he told me the bees Erin and Gaston found were long horned bees."

Gaston barked when he heard his name. Sandra petted him and said, "You're such a clever puppy."

Vlad nodded. "Finding the box was good work, pooch. Dave said long horned bees live underground, not in hives. That box with the smoky smell is a bee cage. Beekeepers use smoke to mask pheromones. Bees warn each other of danger by emitting a scent. Whoever brought the bees into the theater had to have some knowledge of bee behavior."

"When I went to the jewelry store to check out the

surveillance camera, I only saw three people on the footage coming out of the theater," Sandra said. "There was the waiter from Elliot's who told me Victoria gave him a ticket, and this salesman from Fitzgerald's Fine Furniture." She pulled out her cell phone and held it for all to see. "I got his picture here. The balding guy is Larry Treptow."

Norm jumped in. "And I found out Larry Treptow was in line for a promotion at Fitzgerald's until Victoria came back. Then the old man put her in the number one spot. Larry was plenty ticked off about it," Norm's voice rose as he continued. "Now he shows up at the theater, too."

"And with a woman. We've got to find out who he was with!" Beatrice exclaimed.

"Erin said there were five people in the theater when she checked," Vlad held up his hand and touched his fingers as he spoke. "The dead woman is one. The waiter is two. The guy from Fitzgerald's is three, The woman with him is four. But there's still one person unaccounted for." He waggled the last finger at them.

"There's something weird going on at that theater," Sandra said slowly. "Erin saw a strange man on the second floor when she went to get her boss last Friday night to fix the popcorn machine. A spooky man in a glowing tan suit. He pointed at her then he just disappeared," Sandra said. "Her boss tried to convince her it was all in her imagination."

"My daughter is not at all fanciful. If she said she saw a man in a glowing suit, you damn well better believe one was there." Vlad's voice grew strident. "She doesn't exaggerate."

"Wait. There's more." Sandra held up her hand like a traffic cop. "Today he told me about a former manager who lived in an apartment on the second floor for forty years. The poor man was found dead in the sixties."

"This case is growing stranger by the minute." Norm drained the bottle of beer in big gulp. "A woman murdered by bees in a dark movie theater. A mystery woman with a nasty secret. A philandering father. An angry co-worker and now a ghost at the theater. What shit's gonna happen next?"

"We don't have the resources to bring Larry Treptow or Fred Fitzgerald in for questioning. We have no clue who the posh woman is, or who Fred rendezvoused with at Voluptas, or even who the woman with Treptow was on the CCTV." Vlad moved his eyes around the room, holding the gaze of each friend for a second. "We need to gather up the evidence we've collected so far and take it to that police detective."

Sandra gave him a brisk nod. "First, I need get Robert's OK to meet with Detective Johnson. Remember, we have a client to consider." She scrawled a few more notes on the pad.

"Which one of us wants to poke the angry bear?" Beatrice asked. "Detective Johnson kicked Vlad and me out of his office the last time we saw him."

"I only met him once, that night when Gaston tripped the crazy gun toting yoga instructor before she shot Vlad and Beezy. He prob'ly won't even remember me." Norm looked hopeful. "Maybe I should be the one to talk to him, sorta man to man."

Beatrice and Vlad exchanged an alarmed look with each other. "You have no idea what you're up against," Vlad said. "That guy chews hand grenades and spits them out."

"No, if Robert gives his permission, Gaston and I should go to talk to him. We've established a working relationship," Sandra insisted. "Besides, he still owes Gaston and me a dinner for solving Jake Bender's murder."

Gaston sat upright in the recliner and barked.

"Set him straight, Little Buddy. Let him know who's in charge," Norm said. "I just remembered a joke. Ya know what the policeman said to his dinner?"

Gaston barked again, a bit louder.

"Irish Stew in the name of the law."

Chapter Nineteen
No Warmth from this Fuzzy

The young cop working the front desk looked on with a barely repressed smile as Sandra marched into the Crawford police station, Gaston in his shabby service dog harness at her side. She carried a large cloth shopping bag from the Piggly Wiggly store containing Victoria's purse and its contents, the fraudulent letter, and the growing stack of evidence pointing to murder. The cluster of desks behind the reception area held a second female officer working on a computer, so absorbed in her duty that she failed to notice the motley duo.

Although she wore her new power pants suit to the encounter with Detective Johnson, pepper red with a tiny ruffle along the edge and a tasteful black camisole underneath, Sandra's rainbow-colored running shoes seemed to contradict the forceful statement of her suit. She'd found a darling apricot fedora on eBay for forty dollars to complete the look. Gaston trailed behind her, sniffing the grey and tan floor tiles which held the lingering scent of the Crawford police dog, McTuff. The German Shepherd's photo occupied a prominent place on the front desk with the slogan, *Get tough on crime like McTuff.*

"Hello, officer. I'm here to see Detective Johnson," Sandra announced. At the mention of the detective's name, the cop at the front desk's eyes widened with surprise.

"Do you have an appointment?" he asked.

"Please let him know Sandra Tooksbury would like to speak with him. I have some important information I've uncovered in the course of my current investigation." She plopped the shopping bag with the smiling face of a pig wearing a butcher's hat on the counter. "It may shed some light on a woman's mysterious death."

"Let me check if he's available." The young man picked up the phone and pressed a few buttons. "Sir, there's a woman here to see you. Sandra Tooksbury. Says she has some evidence in a murder case to show you…. Yes, she has a poodle with her…Yes, it's still wearing an old service dog harness."

The line crackled with an explosion of colorful language. Sandra couldn't make out what Detective Johnson was saying, but his enthusiastic response was unmistakable. He probably missed working with her after their successful collaboration on the Pickleball Murder, not to mention exposing the extortion attempts involving the victim.

The officer turned to her. "Detective Johnson is in the middle of an important case. He's busy writing up some interviews for the FBI with a crucial deadline. Can you come back tomorrow?"

"Tell him this will only take a few minutes, less than the time it took to arrest Jake Bender's killer after Gaston brought her down." Gaston barked twice, then tugged on his leash in the direction of the back offices. Noticing the confused look on the young cop's face, she explained. "Jake Bender was the pickleball player murdered in the locker room. When his killer's case comes to trial, I'm the star witness."

The cop nodded his head. "I remember interviewing some of the fitness center staff."

"Perhaps you've heard I am also instrumental in bringing down Arthur Aschenbrenner, the romantic scammer who bilked several elderly ladies out of thousands of dollars." Gaston growled deep in his throat at the mention of Arthur's name. "I should have known something was suspicious when my Lovey Puppy tried to bite him." Sandra smiled affectionately at the dog. "He has special abilities when it comes to ferreting out criminals."

Before the officer could respond, the voice on the phone erupted again. "Detective Johnson says to wait here. He's coming to get you," the young cop said.

A grizzly-like man lumbered from the honeycomb of back offices. His rumpled brown suit looked like it had been slept in more than one night. An orange and tan striped tie hung loosely around his neck. His belly hung even looser over belted pants with permanent wrinkles at the waist. He raked five sausage sized fingers through shaggy brown hair pushing it out of his eyes. He said in a gruff voice. "Please follow me."

The lone female officer still working at her desk watched

the unusual procession pass by as the flamboyant elderly lady shuffled behind the bulky officer. Her chubby pooch kept his nose to the floor emitting an occasional loud sniff. The woman officer gave the desk cop a puzzled look. He shrugged his shoulders in a "damned if I know" response.

When they entered his office, the detective gestured to the only chair that wasn't covered with folders. Please take a seat." His massive swivel chair groaned when he sank into it. And grumbled loudly as he leaned forward to rest ham-sized elbows on the desk. He stared at her with tired brown eyes. "What do you have to show me today?"

Sandra settled on the proffered chair, Gaston sitting gingerly on his haunches next to her feet. He fixed his gaze on the policeman, ready to leap to action in a moment's notice. His mistress gave him a reassuring pat before she spoke.

"These are the contents of Victoria Fitzgerald's purse." Sandra withdrew the first ziplocked bag, the flotsam of the victim's belongings clearly visible. She shifted the bag from various angles as she spoke. "As you can clearly see, there's no sign of an epi pen, although everyone who knew her testified she was never without it."

"So she dressed in a hurry and forgot to grab it. Human beings can make mistakes. It's in our nature to have occasional lapses."

"Her fiancé clearly saw her put a new one in her purse." Sandra's eyes blazed with indignation.

Detective Johnson suppressed a yawn. "I know. He was here a few days after her death claiming foul play. As I told the young man, the medical examiner stated she died of anaphylactic shock. One of the most severe reactions to a bee sting that he'd ever seen. Tragic but accidental. I sent him on his way."

Sandra plunked the green purse, also in a clear plastic bag firmly on his desk. "Maybe not so accidental. You could dust for fingerprints on her purse. Somebody stole the epi pen. I'm certain of it. The murderer's fingerprints are on this." She pounded the handbag with her tiny fist. "Just check it out."

"I'm afraid that would be a waste of time and resources. Victoria's death was unfortunate, but I see nothing out of the ordinary. We could have done a complete autopsy if the family requested it, but the Fitzgeralds concurred with the medical examiner. Her father said they almost lost her one other time when she was a teenager. Ended up in the emergency room after a bee stung her at a beach party at Crystal Lake. The lifeguard administered CPR until the EMT's arrived with an epi pen."

"You just proved my point." Sandra shook a knobby finger at him. "Victoria knew a bee sting was a death sentence without access to her epi pen."

"Like I said before, she had a lapse in judgement. Now can I get back to my report?" The detective pushed away from his desk with finality, his eyes lingering on the pile of papers.

Sandra reached in the shopping bag and pulled out the smoky brown box also encased in a zip lock. She dangled it in the air. "What about this? Gaston found it at the movie theater." Gaston rose up to all fours and barked once.

"What the hell is that?" He squinted at the odd-looking wooden box.

Sandra stood and thrust the box toward him. "It's a bee cage. Beekeepers use it to transport queens to a new hive. The murderer used it to bring the killer bees into the movie theater after he stole the epi pen."

Detective Johnson hammered his meaty fist on the desk. "I've heard many crazy theories in my career, but this has to be the craziest. Some anonymous killer steals his victim's epi pen from her purse at a movie theater. Nobody sees anything suspicious when he rummages through her purse. Then he unleashes some killer bees on her, which he's brought with him in a bee cage. They dive bomb her, no one else."

"That's our theory so far. There's other weird happenings at the theater, too. If you'll just test the purse and the bee cage for fingerprints, we'll have a clue to the killer." Sandra placed the bee cage on top of the designer purse.

"If I authorized that, I'd have to have myself tested for a mental illness. The District Attorney would laugh me out of his office if I brought your so-called evidence to his attention. Who the hell would we charge with a set of fingerprints but no suspect?" His brown eyes flashed a warning.

"Isn't it your job to look for suspects and follow the evidence?" Sandra said in a needling tone.

"It's my job to investigate real crimes, not imaginary ones, with no concrete leads." His neck began to turn red as the tendons stuck out.

"We have plenty of leads. Let me show you some of the suspects." She reached into the bag for a still photo of the surveillance camera footage, but he waved her away with his beefy hand.

"Stop right there! I've given you enough of my time," he snarled. "Why can't you watch game shows or *Golden Girls* reruns like other little old ladies? Or take up knitting or crocheting for a hobby? Anything but detective work."

"I'm not about to be put out to pasture like other elderly women when I still have a brain and a purpose. And a dog that's smarter than most humans. Robert Doering came to me for help and I'm not about to let him down. Our team has already uncovered pertinent facts."

"Don't come back to my office until you've got some names and some hard evidence to prove there's been a murder." He clenched his jaw and hissed." I don't have time to indulge in somebody's delusion that she's living an episode of *Murder, She Wrote*."

"Very well. If that's how you want to play it," Sandra sniffed as she retrieved the zip-locked items from his desk and thrust them back into the shopping bag. "I've solved other cases without your help."

"And almost got yourself killed in the process! You can't always depend on your dog to bail you out." He stabbed his finger at her, then shifted his focus back at the heaps of papers on his desk.

"Apparently I can't depend on the police either." Sandra huffed as she moved toward the door.

"Damn, now where did my pen go?" The detective rummaged through some folders on his desk, picking them up and slamming them down. "I don't have time for this shit."

Gaston yipped and put his nose to the ground, snuffling around below the desk. He came up with a black fountain pen in his jaw. He trotted over to the detective and stood on his hind legs, placing front paws on the astonished man's meaty thighs with a slobbering maw. Then he dropped the soggy pen in his lap. He pranced over to Sandra, head held high, tail waving the victory flag as she held the door open for him.

She turned to the detective and said, "This is not the end of the road for our investigation. It's just a bend in the road and I'm going to keep following wherever it leads."

Chapter Twenty
Getting Surly with Surveillance

"That man is an absolute ass!" Sandra declared as she slammed the door to the beat-up Buick, kicking candy wrappers out of her way as she slid in. Gaston yipped from the front seat beside her, then hunkered down, head between paws.

"I take it your meeting didn't go too well," Norm said as he shifted the car into drive and pulled away from the city building. He pushed back the brim of his Green Bay Packers cap to give her a sympathetic wink.

"That's an understatement. I showed him some of the evidence and he told me it was my imagination. Said I should take up knitting or crocheting and stay out of the detective business." The angry huff from her lips sent dust motes careening throughout the car. "I didn't even get a chance to tell him about all the strange stuff going on at the movie theater or show him the suspects from the jewelry store's CCTV camera."

"What do we do now?"

"Let me think." She rubbed her fingers across Gaston's silky ears and he gave an appreciative whine. "We've got the name of one suspect—Larry Treptow. He was at the theater that night and he has a motive. He was angling for a big promotion until Victoria came home. Your friend Cathy said he was really upset."

Norm tapped a finger on the steering wheel. "So we got a name and a face. But we ain't got any reason why he should talk to us. Can't exactly haul him in for questioning."

"I was reading the surveillance chapter in *The Private Detective's Handbook.* If we had the right devices, we could plant a bug in his car or house. Find out what's going on behind closed doors. But we don't have the equipment to do anything like that."

Norm snorted. "Hunh! Fat chance we'd get anywhere near his place without getting caught."

"That's why we're going to park outside Fitzgerald's Furniture and watch. Follow him when he gets in his car. It's called a moving surveillance."

"How we gonna know what car is his?"

"We know what he looks like." She opened the Piggly Wiggly bag and searched through its contents until she found the still photo from the CCTV footage. She laid the picture of the stocky, balding man on the dashboard. "This is Larry Treptow. Look at the hairline and the ski jump nose. I'd recognize him anywhere. We park near the employees' lot and wait for him to leave. Then we tail him."

"Ya mean we're gonna sit outside Fitzgerald's all day?" Norm's voice rose to a squeak. "Ya gotta be kidding."

"If that's what it takes to dig up the dirt on him. He's bound to slip up. We just need to be patient. Have you got a better idea?"

Norm shook his head. "Nope. I got nothing."

"Then let's drive over to Fitzgerald's," Sandra said with a stern set of her jaw. "Find an inconspicuous spot on the street where we can observe the comings and goings and wait."

"We should load up on some food first," Norm said "Who knows how long we'll have to wait. Cops always have sandwiches and coffee when they're on a stake out."

Gaston barked in agreement and they headed to the nearest fast food burger place. There was two-fer special so Norm ordered six cheeseburgers, a large order of fries and two large coffees, with a bottle of water for Gaston. The greasy odor of French fries, coffee, and cheap beef filled the inside of the car. Even Sandra was salivating when Norm handed her the bag and water, placing the two coffee cups in the drink holders between them.

"Ya still carry the pooch's collapsible water dish in yer purse?" He ruffled the curly fur on Gaston's head. "It could be a long day for the little fella."

"Always. I never know when he'll want a drink. Have to keep him hydrated."

Norm pulled over on the street parallel to the parking lot entrance, with a clear view of the favored stalls closest to the employees' door. He aimed the front of the car toward the main intersection and turned the engine off. A row of sleek shiny vehicles formed a barrier near the reserved parking signs. Sandra reached into the bag and handed him two burgers right away, and broke a third into a few pieces, slowly feeding half of them to

Gaston while she munched on the other half. Then she placed a cardboard container of fries on the little ledge below the armrest.

She peered into the bag. "Oops. No Catsup."

"No prob-lay-mo. I can eat 'em plain." He grabbed a handful and munched.

Gaston whimpered, pushing his nose toward the fries. "You know you can't have any. We'll split another burger." She broke off a chunk of burger to distract him.

Norm took a swig from the coffee. "Ya know, I do some of my best thinking over coffee. I tend to have a latte on my mind."

Sandra rolled her eyes and fed another chunk of just the ground beef to the poodle. "Would you like the last burger? Gaston and I have had enough." Before Norm could answer, a man wearing plaid sports jacket and crisply pressed trousers emerged from the factory door. The sun glinted off his shiny pate.

"That's him!" Sandra exclaimed. Her hand shook as she grabbed the picture off the dash, and held it to her nose for a closer look. "That's Larry Treptow. Turn the engine on. He's getting into his car."

Larry Treptow slid into a dark blue Lincoln Continental and slowly backed out of the stall. He turned onto the street in front of them.

"Sweet Jesus! He's coming our way!" Sandra shouted. The man's eyes never glanced in their direction as he guided the gleaming car down the street. Even so, Sandra pulled her peach hat over her face and ducked down in the front seat. Likewise Norm tilted the brim of his cap down, when Larry Treptow drove past.

Once the Lincoln cleared, Sandra clutched at his arm. "Quick, Pull a U-ey! Don't lose him."

Norm gunned the engine and jerked the steering wheel to the left. The car jumped over the curb as he swung quickly around. Coffee splashed into the holders. Then he straightened the car out and they were off. The tires squealed on the pavement. They were in hot pursuit. The duo quickly caught up with the Lincoln but a little green Ford Focus had meandered onto the street in front of them.

"Shit! That other car is in the way." Norm gripped the wheel tightly and craned his head forward intently focused on the blue vehicle.

"It's OK. We don't want to get too close or he'll notice us following him. Use the Ford Focus for cover." Sandra leaned into the passenger side window. "I'll keep a sharp eye out in case he turns off."

Gaston put his front paws on the dashboard and yipped excitedly. Sandra wrapped her arms around him and drew him back. "Careful, Lovey. You don't want to distract Uncle Norm while he's driving,"

Norm carefully kept pace with the two cars as they traveled down several blocks in tandem. "So far, so good." They passed a coffee shop and a row of condominiums. A stoplight loomed in the distance; the green light shone like a beacon. The oncoming traffic was halted waiting for the light to change. Suddenly the Lincoln made a left turn at the intersection while the green Focus sailed on straight ahead. The light changed to yellow. "Hurry up. Don't lose him." Sandra yelped.

Norm stepped on the accelerator. The old Buick lunged forward with a burst of speed that made the engine groan in complaint. The French fries dumped on the floor and the last hamburger spilled out of the fast-food bag. Sandra's new hat flew off her head to the back seat as she tightened her grip around Gaston.

Norm squeaked through as the light turned red. The driver in the first oncoming car shook his fist at Norm, then flashed him the finger. Sandra could see the eff word forming on the angry man's lips.

They had entered a pleasant residential neighborhood, with well-tended yards and newer, upscale houses. A soft grey BMW was parked in a driveway made of pavers. A few houses down, a white Mercedes rested in front of a huge colonial with a three-stall garage.

"Excellent maneuver, Dearie. Fast and furious, just like in the movies." She loosened her hold on Gaston to pat Norm's arm. Norm's heart was still beating fast, adrenalin gushing like a geyser throughout his body. His foot pulsed on the gas pedal. Sweat beads trickled down his forehead and blurred his vision for an instant.

An instant was all it took. Norm failed to notice the turn signal on the Lincoln as it slowed down in front of a magnificent brick two-story. By the time he slammed on the Buick's brakes, he'd clipped the rear end of Larry Treptow's car with a sickening crunch. Norm turned the engine off, and tried to still his rapidly beating heart. The irate man was pounding on his window. Close up, Sandra noticed his broad shoulders and muscular forearms. However, what once was the build of an athlete had gone to pot— too many business lunches over the years.

"Look at what you just did!" Larry Treptow shouted. "What the hell's the matter with you? Didn't you see my turn signal You dented my rear end."

Norm slowly got out of the car and examined the rear end of the Lincoln. The rear driver's side had a long scratch and a small ding.

"I'm real sorry. The sun musta blinded me for a minute," he mumbled.

"What sun?" the man hissed. "It's a cloudy day."

Sandra also emerged from the car with Gaston in her arms. She looked at the Lincoln and clicked her tongue sympathetically. "Oh, dear. It looks like your car got some scratches." Her head bent down as she examined the dusty gray Buick. The rear bumper had absorbed the brunt of the crash with not even a smudge in the film of dirt. She lifted her eyes to Larry's and said, "Not a mark on my car. They don't make them like this anymore."

The fuming man dug a cell phone out of his jacket pocket. "I'm calling the police to report an accident."

Just then a tall long-haired woman in a slinky sapphire blue dress came out of the house. The slit up the side revealed her well-toned thighs and the lowcut bodice enhanced the stunning gems circling her slender neck. From their vivid kaleidoscope of colors and fiery inner light Sandra recognized them as black opals. The woman flipped her lustrous black hair to display the matching opal earrings.

"What's going on, darling?" she purred in a velvety voice. "We're going to be late for lunch at Elliot's. You know we're meeting Serenity and Mother at twelve."

Elliot's. Sandra thought. *Could this be the mystery woman?*

"This fool just ran into our car," Larry sneered. "I'm sorry if we'll be slightly late, Sylvia, but I need to take care of this first. I was about to call the police."

"Let me call my insurance agent," the crafty detective said.

Instead of dialing her insurance company, Sandra snapped a picture of the woman with her phone. "Oh, dear. The line's busy."

She held up open hands. "Do we really need to get the police involved.? They are always so slow to respond. You give me your insurance information and I'll give you mine. My agent will contact you as soon as I get ahold of him."

Larry Treptow frowned at his cell phone. "We need to file an accident report."

"Do we have to do that now?' Sylvia complained. "We're already late. We can stop by the police station after lunch. It's only a few blocks away from the restaurant." She swept her eyes over the damage. "The car isn't that bad." She slid her slender arm through his. "Let's go, darling. My sister traveled a thousand miles for this visit." She tugged him toward the driver's side.

"We'll stop in with our information, too." Sandra promised. "I hope you enjoy lunch. Elliot's food is wonderful." She watched them drive off, then turned to Norm.

"Tomorrow I'm going to show Sylvia Treptow's picture to the nice waiter from Elliot's. Maybe we have the name of the mystery woman after all."

Chapter Twenty-One
All the News There Isn't

Sandra's insurance agent's advice was brief. "Stop by the police station. Show them your license, the insurance card, and the car's title. Don't admit you're at fault. Let me handle the insurance claim with the other company. That's why I'm your agent."

"Thank you so much. You're such a dear man," Sandra said. "My driver isn't certain that fellow had on his signal. I didn't see anything flashing. He made a sudden turn right in front of us."

"When it comes to filing a report, less is more. Keep that in mind," the agent said before he hung up.

Sandra sighed. "I don't think I can face the police again today. Would you please go in and fill out the paperwork?" She removed the necessary documents from the glove compartment and handed them to Norm.

"Ya betcha! I was driving, after all."

While Norm took care of the accident report, Sandra sat waiting in the car with Gaston snoozing on her lap. She called both Vlad and Beatrice and left the same message on their voice mail. "I think we've found the identity of the mystery woman at the theater with Larry Treptow. It's his wife, Sylvia, You can't see her that well on the CCTV feed, but I have an excellent picture of her on my phone. Let's talk after you're done with work."

Sandra stared at the picture of the beautiful Sylvia Treptow, envying the elegant drape of the blue sheath. Her ebony eyes glittered as fiery as the opal necklace in stark contrast with her fine pale complexion, "Lovey Puppy, with the flashy way this woman dresses, people have to notice her. If the waiter can recall seeing her, the people in the movie theater must remember her as well. I'm going to ask Erin when she gets home from school." She gave the sleeping dog a pat and he opened one eye for a second, then lazily shut it again.

He raised his head again when Norm came back and reached over him to return the documents to the glove compartment. The pooch sat up and licked the hand resting on the steering wheel. Norm groused, "I got a lecture about leaving the site of an accident from a cop younger than my jeans, but it's taken care of. Now what?"

"We go home to wait for the rest of the team."

***

Vlad whistled when Sandra showed him the picture of Sylvia. "She must be wearing thousands of dollars' worth of black opals. Chuck Robbins came back from Australia with just one opal like that in a pendant for his wife; claimed he paid three thousand for it."

"She oozes with wealth—designer dress, impeccable make-up, expensive jewelry," Sandra said.

"Cathy said Larry Treptow married the richest woman in Crawford. Sylvia looks the part. I don't get what she sees in him. What a jerk! He gave me holy hell when I accidentally dinged his shiny car." Norm threw his hands up in disgust.

"He had a reason to be angry. You did nail him with the Buick. Anyway I think he may have been good-looking in his younger days, but he let himself go. There are six-pack abs hidden under that blubber," Sandra noted. "I'll take Sylvia's picture to Elliot's tomorrow—see if I can catch the waiter alone. Get his name, too. Just in case we need him for a witness."

"Good idea," Beatrice said. "Can you send her picture to us? I want to print it and take it to Voluptas. Show it to the receptionist. See if she recognizes her at all."

"She dummied up the minute she realized it was Fred Fitzgerald in the photo with Victoria," Vlad said. "She may not want to get involved. Went to great lengths to say she'd get in trouble with her boss if she said another word. Voluptas operates on its reputation for discretion."

"I'll do my best to convince her to talk," Beatrice said.

"No time to be discreet when it's a murder investigation," Sandra grumbled. "That woman needs to get a spine."

"If the receptionist doesn't respond to my appeal to her better angels, maybe I can cudgel her with a few threats to get the police involved. That won't be good for business." Beatrice threw her shoulders back and straightened to all five feet two inches of her height. "If I can handle Florence the Menace at work, I can handle anyone."

Sandra enlarged the picture on her phone and held it up for the group to see. "We need to take her photo to the movie theater and show the staff who worked that night."

Vlad pulled out his phone. "Let me text Erin and find out if she's available." He slid his thumbs over the cell phone as he spoke, "She always answers her text right away. Doesn't want to miss an important message from her friends."

As the team waited for Erin's reply, Norm broke the silence. "That reminds me. I was waiting to see that new movie called "Constipation," but it never came out."

"Puh-leeze, spare us from your dumb jokes," Sandra pleaded.

"Fine. I won't even tell you about the movie with a robot that turns into a tractor. They named it the Transfarmer Movie."

Vlad's phone dinged. He relayed the message to Sandra. "She's working tonight. They're getting the concessions ready. Do you want to go there right now? It'd be a good time to question her co-workers."

Sandra quickly got to her feet from her recliner. "Let me grab my coat. Vlad, would you mind driving me? I think I've had enough thrills with Norm today."

***

The odor of freshly popped corn filled the lobby as Sandra and Gaston entered the theater. Bright lights reflected off the glass display cases on the lobby walls featuring coming attractions. The only familiar name on the posters was Disney. None of the stars tripped the light fantastic in Sandra's memory.

"It looks like Hollywood has passed us by, Lovey," she said to Gaston, "No more rehearsing our act for show biz. We're in the detective business now."

Vlad dropped them off at the door then went to park the car. They slowly made their way across the empty lobby to the concession stand, where Erin and Barb were busy getting ready for the first round of movie goers, minding the popcorn maker and stocking candy on shelves. Gaston yipped a friendly greeting as Sandra said, "The popcorn smells delicious. I'll take a bag to go when we leave."

"Hi, Auntie Sandra," Erin said. "You remember Barb?"

"Yes, I do, Dearie. I never forget a kind face," she said. "How's it going?"

"It's Thursday, usually a slow night," the older woman replied. "Erin gets to leave after the first showing and I'm doing clean up."

"Did Erin mention we're private detectives?" Sandra lowered her voice in a conspiratorial tone. "We're investigating the death of Victoria Fitzgerald after her fiancé requested our help."

"She said you'd be stopping by with a woman's picture— to see if we recognize her from that night. I was pretty busy, it was a Friday and we had two opening shows. But I'll give it a shot." Barb wiped her hands on a towel and leaned over the counter. "I've been making popcorn. The oil gets a little greasy," she said apologetically.

Sandra set her purse on the counter and dug out her phone. She scrolled through her photos until she came to Sylvia's picture. She set it on the counter with a hopeful expression.

Barb picked it up and studied it carefully. "She looks familiar. Probably been in the theater before. Everybody in town passes through here sooner or later. I can't say definitely that I saw her that night. Like I said, we were busy."

She handed the phone to Erin.

"I saw her!" Erin said excitedly. "She was here that night with some man. They were arguing about the movie. I remember because there weren't many people coming out and I was doing clean-up. Only she looked different. No jewelry. Wore a long coat with a hood.'

"Do you think you can identify the man if I show you some footage from Mr. Bradley's CCTV camera?"

"Yes. I'll never forget that night." Erin gave a little shiver.

"Wow, CCTV footage. That's so cool. Just like one of those cop shows." Barb's voice was filled with awe.

"Only it's real and deadly serious," Vlad said as he approached the counter. "Was there anyone else working who might have seen this couple?"

"Henry was working, but he was in the projection room. Mark was cleaning the lobby and helping out with tickets, He definitely could have seen them," Erin said.

"Is Mark here?" Sandra glanced around.

Barb pointed to the staircase. "Both are upstairs."

"Vlad, can you please take my phone up there? I don't think I can climb those stairs after the day I had. It's a wonder I didn't get whiplash." Sandra handed him the cell phone.

"I'll go with you, Dad. It's kind of confusing up there," Erin offered. "Is that ok with you, Barb?"

"Sure, honey. I want to talk to your Auntie Sandra." Barb leaned over the counter and whispered, "I read in the *Daily Gazette* about that guy who was murdered after a pickleball game. Rumor going around he was laying naked on the locker room floor. Is it true he was strangled with some peacock boa?"

"I can't divulge information about an ongoing case," Sandra said hastily, wincing at the thought of her feather boa used as a murder weapon. "But I can tell you how my dog captured some jewel thieves when we were on a Rhine River cruise."

Sandra flicked her finger. Gaston rose on his hind legs and performed a little dance. Both Erin and Barb clapped while Vlad rolled his eyes with a tight-lipped grimace.

"That adorable little dog caught some jewel thieves? Tell me more," the concession worker begged.

While the two women were busily chatting, Erin led Vlad up the creaky stairs. "Careful, Dad," she warned. "There's a tear in the carpet on the top step. It's easy to get your toe snagged and trip."

At the head of the stairs, Vlad halted and gaped at the naked torso of the mannequin in the flickering light of the overhead bulb, its bare legs pointed toward them. "What the heck is that?" he said.

"It's the bottom half of the dummy in the box office," she replied.

They walked carefully around the stacks of empty reels and boxes of old movie paraphernalia. Chewbacca waved his floppy cardboard arm as they strode past. A rustling sound from behind the stacks of old posters startled Vlad and he grabbed Erin's shoulder. The moldy smell of damp walls caused him to sneeze. His eyes started watering. Fortunately, Mark's office door was open and they heard the murmur of male voices and a welcoming light.

Suddenly Sandra shouted up the stairs, "Come back, Gaston."

The clicking of Gaston's nails clattered on the steps. Gaston's curly head appeared at the top of the stairway. His yips echoed throughout the dimly lit hallway. The poodle darted into the piles of boxes with an ominous growl. He grabbed an old poster of John Wayne with his teeth and dragged it out of the pile, shaking it and growling.

"Stop that!" Vlad shouted. He tried to grab the leash. The dog dropped the poster and scurried back to the pile of trash, thrusting his head in once more. This time he clutched a dusty wallet in his mouth as he trotted up to Vlad and deposited at his feet, looking up with a lolling tongue and a pleased expression in his eyes.

"What's this, buddy?" Vlad bent down to retrieve the leather billfold. He opened it to see who it belonged to. A folded-up faded newspaper clipping fell out. Vlad saw a long-expired driver's license issued to Henry Radke. Erin picked up the newspaper, unfolded it and read the headlines, "Boating Accident Claims Life of Teen."

"This article is from June, 1989. Listen to this, Dad. 'An afternoon of high school hijinks ended in tragedy when Rachel Radke, age 15, daughter of Roy and Selma Radke drowned in the Rock River. A group of teenagers celebrated the last day of school with a party that involved underage drinking. Fred Fitzgerald, Jr. told police they were playing a drinking game of truth or dare when Rachel lost the dare and had to dive off the Riverview Park pier. When she didn't surface, he dove in after her, but the strong current and muddy bottom made a rescue impossible.'"

"What are you doing with my old wallet?" a voice behind them thundered. Henry snatched the billfold from Vlad and glared at him and Erin. "I lost it years ago."

"Our dog found it in the pile of old movie posters." Vlad murmured. "We didn't know who it belonged to until we looked inside."

The man's face darkened, twisting with anger until he resembled an ancient gargoyle. "Who gave you permission to snoop in my belongings!" He ripped the yellowed newspaper from Erin's hand. "God damn it! You have no business reading that. It's personal."

Mark followed close on Henry's heels. "What's going on?"

"These two busybodies were prying into my personal stuff."

"Gaston heard a noise behind the boxes and he came out with this billfold. We didn't know who it belonged to." Erin's voice trailed off.

"Was that the one you lost when you first started working here? That's got to be twenty-five years ago," Mark said.

"It doesn't matter. They had no right to read my personal papers."

"We're very sorry. We didn't know…" Erin's feeble voice trailed off.

'Humph!" The angry man snorted. "You still had no right, no right at all."

"This is all a misunderstanding. You got your wallet back," Mark said. "That's the main thing. You better check the computer to make sure the first feature is ready to go." He patted Henry on the shoulder. "I'm sorry, man. I know how hard your sister's death was on your family. Let's get back to work."

He watched Henry shuffle off, then turned to the father and daughter team standing in the dark hall. "Erin, what are you and your dad doing up here?"

"It's nothing, Mark," Vlad said quickly. "I had a question for you, but we can talk another time. You have a movie to get ready."

Before Erin could say a word, he whisked her and Gaston down the stairs.

chapter Twenty-Two
His Sister Rachel

"What was Henry yelling about?" Barb asked. "We could hear him down here like he was standing next to us."

"We found an old billfold of his," Erin said. "A newspaper clipping fell out. He had a sister who drowned. Seemed pretty upset about it. Snatched it out of my hand. Even swore at me."

"That would've been his sister Rachel. She died years ago at a teen-age drinking party. Fred Junior brought the beer and cheap wine." Barb lowered her voice and looked around conspiratorially. "Some people said Junior had a crush on her but she refused to go out with him. So he got her drunk at the party, hoping she'd give in. The other kids said the poor girl dove in the water to get away from him. She must have hit some rocks on the bottom and never surfaced. Supposedly Fred Junior jumped in after her. There was always some doubt whether he tried to save her or held her under. A bunch of drunken young kids weren't very reliable witnesses."

"The newspaper said it was due to a drinking game gone bad," Vlad said.

'Yeah, that's what the cops wanted everyone to believe. No one wanted to mess with the biggest employer in town at the time."

"You mean Fitzgerald's Fine Furniture was a major operation?" Vlad raised his eyebrow. "Doesn't seem like there's a big demand for custom office furniture."

"No! Fred Senior had a big mattress factory. He sold that off to a major corporation for a huge amount of money and switched to the custom-made stuff. Bigger profits and less headaches, according to him. But the Radke family always believed there was a cover-up and Fred Junior got off scot-free."

"So Henry inherited the family's resentment of the Fitzgerald's," Sandra said.

"Henry was just a kid when his sister died, but his mother never really got over it. She started drinking to numb the pain. His teachers tried to get social services involved but Henry's father slammed the door in the social worker's face when she came to check on the situation."

"He probably has a lot of repressed anger," Vlad observed. "That explains his reaction to Erin's reading the old newspaper account."

Barb nodded her head in agreement. "Most of the time, Henry acts like a clueless idiot, prattling on about dumb stuff, like whether cheese curds or pickles are better deep fried. But there's a mean streak that raises its ugly head once in a while."

"Is that why Mark seems to walk on eggshells around him?" Erin asked.

"Nah, Mark's just a naturally considerate guy. He wouldn't hurt a fly. He's put everything he's got into keeping this theater going." Barb sighed. "Believe me it hasn't been easy. The multiplex at the mall is stiff competition. The owner would love to see the Classic Cinema fold. Then they'd have a monopoly and could raise prices on the movies and concessions. Mark's standing in the way of their profits."

"I'm sure the folks in Crawford appreciate how Mark's managed to keep the ticket prices low," Vlad observed. "Plus all he does for community groups, like showing an old-time movie to raise money for the children's hospital foundation." Vlad pointed to a poster advertising the upcoming event. "That's got to eat into the profits a bit."

"When all the movie studios switched to digital, Mark couldn't afford to buy the new equipment. The whole town pitched in with fundraisers to save the Classic. Mark put the pictures of everyone who made a contribution on a video and showed it before the coming attractions for months."

"He seems like a hell of a guy," Vlad said.

He's a great boss," Erin added. "A lot nicer than the manager of the Aquatic Center concessions stand, where I worked last summer. She was a grouch. I don't think she liked kids very much."

"Not to mention he has the best popcorn in town," Sandra said, munching the buttery treat as she listened to the conversation. "Right, Gaston?" She tossed him a freshly popped morsel which he caught mid-air and swallowed. Then the little dog barked in appreciation.

"He sure is one smart pup!" Barb laughed. "Next time you bring him in, the popcorn's on me."

Chapter Twenty-Three
Rule of Three

"There's something that's been bothering me since my conversation with your boss. I just can't recall exactly what he said that day," Sandra said to Erin when she and Vlad picked her up after her shift. She folded her hand in a prayer position and tapped her lips with her index fingers as she thought. "It was something about the run of bad luck at the theater."

"I know Barb doesn't like to go up to the second floor. She says it's because of her knees acting up, but she seems to move just fine when she works the concessions. I figured," Erin shrugged, "she believes there's a creepy guy in a tan suit wandering around up there and doesn't want to run into him." The girl put her arms around Gaston who snuggled next to her on the back seat. "She's a little superstitious. Right, Gaston?" The pooch let out a happy little "erf" and rested his head on her lap.

"Mark told me about the ghost story connected to the man in the tan suit," Sandra said absentmindedly. "But that's not what's bothering me."

"Ghost story? What do you mean, a ghost story?" Erin's voice grew shrill as she sat upright. "Mark told me the man in the tan suit was all my imagination!"

Her sudden movement disturbed the dozing dog and he complained with a little moan.

"Oh dear. He didn't want the tale to get out," the old lady murmured. "He was afraid people would stop coming to the theater if they thought it was haunted. He asked me not to repeat what he said."

Vlad gave Sandra a sideways glance. "Now you have to tell both of us. Even my curiosity is aroused."

"Yeah, Auntie Sandra. Spill the beans!" Erin demanded.

Sandra hesitated before she carefully spoke. "Did you know there's an apartment on the second floor? Behind Chewbacca and all the old posters and cut outs?"

"No. Mark always told us it was just an old storeroom," Erin said.

"A man named Oscar O'Brian, the original manager, lived there for forty years. Another employee found him dead in that apartment. Rumors spread around town that he loved the theater so much he didn't want to leave so he's haunting it. No one has touched the apartment since they found him lying there. He supposedly is the man in the tan suit."

Erin's eyes grew wide. "So I did see a ghost!"

"Mark said it's just a rumor. He never saw any man in a tan suit in all the years he's been manager. But other people claim to have seen something. He doesn't want the story to get out—afraid he'll lose customers. The Classic operates on a tight budget."

Vlad commented, "He could always raise prices. Four bucks is pretty cheap for a first run movie, even if it is a little past its opening."

"You mean a lot past its release," Erin said. "Plus, the community wouldn't like that since they worked so hard to save the theater."

"There was something else. He said bad luck always comes in threes but I can't remember what the other unfortunate event was." She scratched her head, then gave it a hard shake. "Getting old is the pits. If I didn't have Gaston to keep me on top of things, I'd be in a sorry state."

Gaston yipped in agreement.

"I bet Barb will know. I can bring it up with her when concessions gets slow and it's just us two," Erin said excitedly.

Vlad pulled into the driveway of his former home. The yard light was on. He could see the flashing images on the television screen through the brightly lit living room window. Maria must be waiting up for Erin. "Are you sure you want to be involved in the investigation? Your mother will not be happy if she thinks I dragged you into this. You know how she feels about Gaston and Auntie Sandra." He gave Sandra an apologetic smile. "I'm sorry, Sandra, but I have to remind her of Maria's temper, lest she forget how long her mother's tantrums last when she gets angry."

"No offense taken. Gaston and I have had worse things said about us." Sandra waved his concerns away with the flick of her hand.

Erin piped up from the back seat." I'm already involved, Dad. I found the murder victim and I saw the ghost. I just won't tell Mom what I'm up to." The teen rolled her eyes. "What she doesn't know can't hurt her."

"Dearie, be careful. Detective work can be dangerous." Sandra warned. "I've had some close calls. If not for Gaston, I shudder to think what might have happened."

Vlad frowned, his eyebrows hitched into a knot. "Questioning Barb might not be such a good idea. Word gets out very fast in a small town. Gossip is the main entertainment for some people."

Erin gently removed Gaston from her lap as she slid toward the car door. "Don't worry. I'll be careful. It's only a harmless little talk with Barb. Good night. I love you guys." She blew them an air kiss but avoided making eye contact with both of the adults.

Vlad and Sandra exchanged a worried look as the girl slammed the door. "She's your daughter. Smart and fearless."

"Foolhardy more like it." Vlad sighed.

Erin paused before she entered her house, unwilling to face another round of her mother's nagging. Her mind was racing. *Mark's been keeping secrets. What else is going on that I don't know about? A dead guy used to live in a secret apartment on the second floor. There's bound to be some clues in there. Maybe I'll find out if the man in the tan suit is real.*

She shivered, but this time with excitement as she plotted how to get into the supposed storeroom on the second floor. Her nose wrinkled with concentration as she considered ways to get Mark out of his office so she could snoop around upstairs.

Chapter Twenty-Four
Back to The Love Shack

Vlad watched as Sandra and Gaston slowly made their way up her driveway. The flickering shadows of the trees swaying under the streetlights warned of another restless night. He didn't like Erin's involvement in this investigation. He wanted to protect all his children from the evils of the world as long as possible, but this time evil sought his daughter out. Was her agency more important than her safety? The sinking feeling in his stomach threatened to shipwreck his evening. The longing for Beatrice's comforting touch prompted him to call her.

"May I come over? There's been some new developments I'd like to discuss."

"I was just about to text you. I have some unfinished business we need to take care of."

Vlad hoped the unfinished business involved testing out the pillow top mattress. What was the optimal level of firmness? No matter. He'd rise to the occasion. Breaking all speed records to get to her house, he pictured her in her black silky negligee, nipples peeking through the lace bodice.

Beatrice answered the door wearing joggers and a faded Crawford U sweatshirt, not dressed for the pursuits which he envisioned on the drive over. Even worse, her nasty tuxedo cat, Max, hissed menacingly when he stepped in the entry way. The cat glared at him with flinty yellow eyes and ears laid back, in an imitation of a Siberian tiger on the hunt.

Vlad never criticized any of her choices, either in clothing or pets. Hadn't she chosen him out of all the single men at the university? He only felt gratitude that she had persisted in loving him after Maria kicked him out, when his foolish fumbling with a sexy co-ed, and his involvement with a student protest movement and the ruthless terrorist behind it almost destroyed his career. Ignoring the cat, he gathered her in his arms, planting a long, lingering kiss on her lips.

"Wow! That must be some exciting development!" she said when they came up for air. "I can't wait to hear what's caused this reaction."

"I really needed to see you tonight." He led her to the couch and pulled her down next to him, draping his arm around her shoulders. Max jumped up on the opposite upholstered chair and stared, eyes narrowed and tail twitching. "Sandra told us about some weird happenings at the theater that she found out from the manager. But Mark wouldn't go into all the details. Erin wants to pump her coworker, Barb, for more information. I'm not certain I like my daughter getting even more involved."

"It's only talking, right? Plus she's on the inside. None of us can get information like she can without arousing suspicion."

"I suppose. If you think she'll be all right…"

"I'm sure she'll be careful. She's a sensible girl."

"What was the unfinished business to which you were referring? Obviously, it doesn't involve modeling your new black nightie." Vlad nuzzled her neck and began nibbling gently on her ear.

"It might." Beatrice said in a breathy voice. "What do you think about making a little visit to Voluptas?"

Vlad groaned, "Oh yes. Satin sheets and our own hot tub!" His kisses grew deeper, until Beatrice puled away and sat upright.

"First we make sure Desiree is manning reception," she said. "Then we show her Sylvia Treptow's picture. I'm dying to know if she's our mystery woman."

"So is Sandra. She's going to check with the waiter at Elliot's. Find out if Sylvia was the woman arguing with Victoria."

"If Desiree confirms Sylvia and Fred are doing the nasty, we have another suspect. Victoria finds out her dad is having an affair with the assistant manager's wife and gets irate. Threatens to tell her husband. Sylvia would have a good reason to shut her up."

"Let's do it tomorrow! I have something else in mind for today. But first, can you please lock your cat in the laundry room? I don't want to expose any sensitive parts of my body to his claws."

***

The second journey to Voluptas unfolded on a balmy late September day with a cloudless blue sky. An invigorating romp with Beatrice the previous night restored his positive outlook.

Occasionally she reached out and massaged the back of his neck. His hunched-up shoulders relaxed under her gentle touch. She rested her tiny hand wearing their engagement ring on his thigh. He gave a quick squeeze to her fingers and returned his hand promptly to the two o'clock position on the steering wheel.

The same looping driveway led to the gracious white building nestled in the rolling hills. Beatrice grabbed her briefcase from the backseat and strode boldly up the path to the entrance. Bees buzzed around the deep purple blooms of the asters growing along the sidewalk. Vlad observed, "Even an innocent creature like a bee can be turned into a murder weapon. People can be so devious."

"I have a feeling we're getting closer to uncovering the killer." Beatrice's voice hardened. "Whoever devised the perfect crime wasn't counting on us getting involved."

After opening the doors for Beatrice to enter before him, Vlad studiously avoided looking at the artwork in the lobby. He kept his eyes fixed on the backs of the middle-aged couple in a deep discussion with the receptionist, Desiree. The twill trousers slid off the man's flat buttocks, held in place by a tooled brown belt. The woman's sequin-encrusted jacket covered her ample hips. The pink and purple horse's head painted on the back seemed to be winking at him. A girlish giggle echoed through the nearly empty lobby as the man muttered something in her ear.

Desiree smiled encouragingly at the couple as she twirled a long lock of her hair around her finger. She rattled off a polished sales pitch highlighting the features of an upgraded room, pointing to the small swimming pool in a brochure spread out before them. The man whistled, then declared, "We'll go for it. Give us the best you got. We're celebrating the final decree of my divorce."

The woman twittered. "Might as well spend the money before she lays her mitts on it."

Handing them a room card, Desiree said, "There's a gratis bottle of champagne chilling in the ice bucket, to show our appreciation. We have a delicious room service menu. The bathroom is stocked with whatever lotions and gels you may desire. If you open anything, you will be charged for it, however. Consider them yours to take with you."

The man grabbed the woman's hand and they mooned at

each other like lovesick teenagers, crooning 'snookums' and 'you sweet thing' ad nauseum. The woman's jacket fell open to reveal her ample cleavage in a low necked purple top. Her push-up bra was working overtime. Before Desiree could finish her spiel, they waved her off and galloped down the hallway in search of their upgraded room, overnight bags in hand.

The receptionist's wide smile turned upside down when she saw Vlad and Beatrice. She graced them with a cold hard stare before giving a frosty greeting. "How may I help you?" She thrust the brochure out of sight and picked up a pen. Her knuckles grew white as she gripped the pen tightly. Vlad feared it would snap in two and spray the desk with ink.

Beatrice smiled sweetly and said cordially, "How nice to see you again, Desiree. We were here a week or so ago, inquiring about Victoria Fitzgerald. Somehow, we were under the impression she had an account here."

Desiree spoke in a clipped voice. "I remember. You were mistaken. We had no record of Victoria Fitzgerald ever staying here."

"Oh, yes. We showed you a picture and you identified her father, Fred Fitzgerald, as a frequent visitor. But the woman with him was not the woman in the photograph. I brought another photo for you to take a look at."

"I told you last time. I'm not allowed to give out information on any of our guests. We have strict confidentiality rules." She slammed the pen down. "I could lose my job if I breech protocol."

"I'm not just a lawyer. I'm also a private investigator," Beatrice said. Vlad's eyes widened with surprise as she continued in her Matlock voice. "We are working on a very important case. A murder investigation. I need you to look at this woman and tell me if you've seen her here before." She placed her briefcase on the reception desk and took out the photo of Sylvia Treptow. "Do you recognize her?"

"I'm sorry. I can't help you." Desiree slowly lifted her hands palms up in a helpless gesture.

"Perhaps you'd rather I turn my evidence over to the police?" Beatrice's steely eyed stare caused the young woman's posture to wilt. "Would you prefer to talk to an officer of the law?

I can imagine what kind of a reaction your guests would have when they see a police car pull up."

Desiree looked wildly about, then gave a furtive glance at the door marked 'office.' It remained closed. She leaned closer to Beatrice, swallowed hard, and studied the picture of Sylvia. Finally she spoke. "She's the one. The woman who came here with the older man. They've been here several times, always checking in under his name."

Beatrice nodded approvingly. "Thank you for your cooperation. We'll try to be discreet as we continue our investigation." She placed the picture back inside the folder, snapped shut the briefcase and turned to Vlad. "We'd best head back to the city. It's a long drive."

After a silent walk through the lobby and back down the path, Vlad let out a whoosh of air. "What the hell! First, you're a lawyer, and now a private detective. I could hardly believe my ears."

Tossing her briefcase onto the backseat. Beatrice smiled. "I might as well be damned for two lies as well as one. At least now we know Sylvia's dirty little secret. I can't wait to tell Sandra."

Chapter Twenty-Five
Erin the Sidekick

The next morning Sandra washed down her vitamins and calcium supplements with an energy drink. "I'm going to need a big boost for what we've got planned for today," she said to Gaston. "But first, I want to talk to Erin. I didn't like the look on that girl's face when she left the car. She's up to something. I'm not going to let her get into trouble on her own."

Gaston ran into the bedroom and came out with his sock monkey. Like a wolf going in for the kill, he growled and gave it a fierce shake. His floppy ears swished side to side like a crazed metronome until he sat back on his haunches and dropped it at her feet.

"I know, Lovey Puppy. I'm ready for action, too. I'm going to text Erin and find out the next time she goes into work. I have a plan."

Sandra texted: *Please call me today. Make sure you're alone. Don't tell your Dad. We need to talk.* She stirred some Metamucil into her orange juice and waited for the teen's response.

She didn't have long to wait. Around eleven thirty, Erin called. "I'm calling from a stall in the girl's bathroom. No Dad here. What's up?"

"When do you work at the theater again?"

"Tomorrow night." The teen hesitated for a moment before she spoke. "Why do you ask?"

"Will Barb be working?"

"Barb works every night except Monday and Tuesday. The theater is closed on those two days."

"Is Mark ever there alone on those days?"

"Yeah, he counts the ticket sales and concessions totals on Monday."

"Does he keep the doors locked?"

"Usually the front doors are always open when he's there. He likes to be available in case someone wants to rent the theater.

All of the fundraisers are scheduled for Tuesday nights. He pays Barb and Henry overtime to come in."

Sandra's mind was racing faster than the Metamucil through her intestines. She spoke quickly.

"What if your ailing Auntie Sandra needs someone to accompany her to her doctor's appointment on Monday and you're the only person available? Could you get out of school?"

"Yeah, if I have an excuse from Mom or Dad. Why? What's up?"

"I think you and I need to pay a visit to the storeroom. When you left the car last night, you were thinking of sneaking in there. Weren't you? Be honest."

"Yes, kinda," Erin said reluctantly. "I didn't know how I was going to pull it off, but I was going to try."

Sandra got up from the kitchen table and began pacing around the room with Gaston at her heels. "I have an idea. We're going to need Uncle Norm's help. Monday afternoon, when Mark's alone. Can your parents call in an excuse or does it have to be written?"

"You can call the attendance office in the morning, but we will need something written the next day."

"We'll worry about a written excuse later. It's easier to beg forgiveness afterwards than to ask permission before. I'll take complete responsibility."

"No worries. I can write just like my mom. I've forged her signature before when she forgot to sign a permission slip for a field trip and I needed to turn it in that day. You leave the message on attendance and I'll take care of the rest."

"That's my girl!"

"When I go to work tomorrow, I'll pump Barb for the third unfortunate event just like in that book by Lemony Snickett."

Next Sandra called Norm. "Remember when I told you about my conversation with Mark, the theater manager? He told me about the previous manager who lived on the second floor and died in his apartment. Now it's a storeroom. Erin and I are going to check it out on Monday. But we're going to need your help."

"Why me? You're the one who picks locks. If you're going to keep up this breaking and entering gig, you really should get a gun. You know why?"

"To protect myself. I suppose."

"No. That's not it. Most burglars are armed, because armless burglars can't get away with much."

Sandra groaned. "If you keep this up, I'm going to have to replace you with a new sidekick.

***

"That's a relief," Sandra said to Gaston after the Metamucil did its job. "Time to get dressed for a late lunch and you're coming with me, Lovey Puppy."

After pulling on her peacock blue tunic and matching satin pants, she draped a rhinestone and silver necklace over her head and sighed. The police had returned the beautiful peacock feather boa from the evidence bag, but Sandra just couldn't bring herself to wear it yet. It was the weapon used to strangle the victim in the pickleball murder case. Looking at it now brought her no pleasure. She should ask Vlad to help her sell it on E-bay and give the proceeds to victims of a sexual abuse non-profit.

"Come here, Puppy," she called to Gaston. He meekly submitted to the service dog harness and they were ready to go. She called Norm and they drove off to Elliot's Inn. She had checked yesterday and the young, long-haired waiter would be working this noon hour.

When Norm dropped them off at the entrance, he said, "So glad you're going to a fancy restaurant today, Little Buddy, Bone Appetit!"

The same cranky hostess stuffed into the dirndl glared at them when they entered. She started to say, "No dogs ..." but quit when she saw the words on Gaston's harness.

Sandra flashed her best little old lady smile. "I hope you're still serving lunch. I know it's after two thirty, but I had a doctor's appointment that ran late. I'm practically starving."

"The kitchen switches to the dinner menu at three. You can still get lunch if the chef hasn't run out." The hostess sulked as she reluctantly led them to a table in the darkest corner of the empty restaurant. "As you can see, the lunch crowd has left,' she said plopping down a menu. The young waiter soon appeared to take their order.

"Nice dog," he said. "My aunt had a poodle once, but she was full size and black."

"This is Gaston," Sandra said. Gaston yipped in a friendly greeting. "But that's not why I'm here. I figured now is a good time to talk."

"You got that right. It's usually slow until five. What's up?"

"Remember a few weeks ago, when you overheard an argument between Victoria Fitzgerald and a woman."

The waiter nodded.

Sandra continued, "I'm wondering if you could take a look at this photo and tell me if this is the woman you saw."

"Sure thing. I'd never forget a hottie like that." The young man grinned. "Not too many lookers like her come into this place."

Sandra retrieved her phone from her purse and found the picture of Sylvia Treptow. She held it out to the waiter. "Is this the woman?"

He gave a low whistle. "That's her, all right. She had on the same earrings and necklace, too. Musta cost some big bucks."

"Thank you for your assistance. If we need to get the police involved, would you be willing to identify her for the record?" Sandra asked, imploring him with her piercing blue eyes.

"Yes, ma'am. Miss Fitzgerald was one of my biggest tippers. I miss her a lot. You can count on me to help."

"Excellent, young man. Could you please write your name and address on this page?" She pulled out the spiral she labeled her casebook and watched the young man print Sydney Greene and a local address. Tucking the notebook back into her bag, she continued, "Now I'd like to order your best steak for my dog and me. I'll have some of your delicious rolls and a side salad."

After the waiter left to place her order with the kitchen, Sandra texted Beatrice: *Sylvia Treptow is definitely the mystery woman from the restaurant. Now it's your turn to check out the secret love nest.*

Beatrice texted back: *Already on it. Driving back from Voluptas. Receptionist confirmed Sylvia was shacking up with Fred Fitzgerald. Let's meet to decide how to proceed.*

Chapter Twenty-Six
Interview with a Vamp

When Vlad and Beatrice arrived at Sandra's house after their stop at Voluptas, Norm and Sandra were already enjoying their adult beverages. Sandra reclined in her Lazy girl, her feet clad in her fuzzy pink slippers, while Norm cozied up to Gaston on the sofa.

"Martinis are ready and waiting in the cocktail shaker. Please pour yourself one and join us." Sandra gestured toward the credenza where the silver shaker and two empty glasses stood.

While his fiancée settled in on the love seat, Vlad poured the two drinks, then brought them over to her. Beatrice related what happened at Voluptas. "I felt dishonest about saying I was a lawyer, but I figured the end justifies the means, Besides, we are private detectives. Isn't Robert Doering a paying client?" Her green eyes glowed with pride.

"That's what I've been saying all along, Dearie," Sandra agreed. "I just need to apply for my license in the state of Wisconsin to make it legal. I checked on the requirements. I'm sure I qualify."

"The only thing I qualify for is the state of confusion," Norm said. "But I have my little buddy here to steer me straight." He gave Gaston a pat on the head. "A second Sherlock Hounds."

"Let's summarize what we learned about Sylvia so far," Vlad said. "Victoria threatened to tell about her secret at the restaurant. Desiree identified her as the woman carrying on with Fred Fitzgerald. Since Pat Bradley recognized Larry Treptow in the surveillance tape, she most likely attended the movie with him. Evidence is piling up."

"But most of it is circumstantial." Beatrice shrugged. "We need something more solid."

"If Sylvia's fingerprints are on the bee cage or Victoria's purse, we'd have her dead to rights," Norm exclaimed. "We just gotta get the police to run some tests."

"That's a big ask. Detective Johnson wasn't too eager to get involved." Sandra used the remote to lower her feet. Then she stood up and said. "First, I'd like to talk to her and take Gaston with me. He's a great judge of character."

When the poodle heard his name, he jumped off the couch and dashed to her side. Standing on his hind legs, Gaston gave a little bark.

"See. He's ready to investigate," Sandra said proudly. She pulled a dog treat from her pocket and tossed it. The pooch snatched it mid-air and gulped it down.

"He's ready for my Bud and Viv story." Norm took a swig from his beer. "All this talk about shacking up reminded me of the time when they wanted to celebrate their fiftieth anniversary."

Gaston barked again.

"Uncle Bud turned to Auntie Viv and asked, 'Whaddya want to do to celebrate our anniversary? Viv gave him a sexy look and answered, 'Let's run upstairs and make love.' He said, "Well makeup yer mind. I can't do both.'"

Beatrice chuckled. "When you said 'both' I got an idea. Both Sandra and I will visit Sylvia. Sandra knows where she lives because of the accident."

"I can drive ya there," Norm volunteered. "I remember the way."

"We have the address from the accident report," Sandra went to the credenza and held up some papers. "It might be better if only Beatrice and I went. She has all that practice in talking like a lawyer."

"We'll time it right after Larry goes to work. Sylvia should be alone. I'll pose as your insurance agent until she lets us in the door."

Sandra's eyes flashed with excitement. "We'll stake out the house early in the morning. Watch until the husband leaves. Then we'll swoop in. Sylvia won't stand a chance with us double teaming her."

***

At seven o'clock the next morning, Beatrice picked up coffee and muffins at Kwik Stop, and brought some Pork Chomp treats for Gaston. Sandra tapped her fingers nervously on the arm rest as the younger woman parked the car around the corner with a good view of the Treptows' house. She peeked into the bag with the bakery and said, "I'm too excited to eat." She slurped the coffee, setting it down in the coffee holder. "We're just like Cagney and Lacey. I can't decide if I'm beautiful like Cagney or smart like Lacey. Maybe I'm both."

Gaston rose on his hind legs, pressing his nose against the passenger window. They didn't have long to wait until the garage door opened and the big blue Lincoln Continental streaked out. The pooch yipped when the car drove by.

"Are you ready to tackle Sylvia Treptow?" Sandra asked.

"You bet. Let's roll." Beatrice started up the engine and cruised to the suspect's driveway.

Sylvia took some time before she answered the doorbell. She padded to the door in her bare feet toes painted dusky rose. The bright red lipstick and shimmering eye shadow enhanced her flawless complexion. The pale blue leotard clung to all the curves of her body. Her dazzling smile faded when she recognized Sandra. "Oh it's you," her lips fell into a pout. "What do you want?"

"May we come in, dearie? There's still a few insurance questions my agent would like to ask you."

"I suppose," she said reluctantly. "But make it quick. My Body Flow class starts in forty-five minutes.

As Beatrice and Sandra stepped inside, she noticed Gaston. "Does the dog have to join us? The house has undergone some renovations and we have new carpeting. I don't want some mongrel to make a mess." She waved her hand at a living room belonging to a photo shoot from a *House Beautiful* magazine,

"Not to worry. He's a well-trained service dog," Sandra reassured her. "I'm prone to seizures and he gives off an early warning when one is about to come on."

Sylvia's widened with alarm. "Seizures? I don't know how to respond to a health emergency."

"Don't worry. I do," Beatrice smiled brightly as she lowered herself onto a peach leather sofa and opened her briefcase. She pulled out the police report. "It says here you witnessed the accident."

"I was there, if you consider my presence as a witness."

The woman perched precariously on the arm of a love seat. Sandra sat next to her and surreptitiously turned on her cell phone to record the conversation. Gaston watched the proceeding with a wary eye.

Beatrice pretended to shuffle some papers." I see you have been present around town in several questionable pursuits."

"What on earth are you referring to? What kind of an insurance agent are you anyway?" Sylvia's face clouded with suspicion.

Sandra jumped in. "I'll get right to the point. My associate and I are private detectives. A few weeks ago Robert Doering came to see us. His fiancé, Victoria Fitzgerald, died from anaphylactic shock due to a bee sting. The police ruled it as accidental, but he disagreed."

"So I heard. My husband works at Fitzgerald's and came home with the sad news." She glanced at her perfectly manicured hand. "That has nothing to do with me. Why are you telling me all this?"

"Because you were overheard arguing with the victim at Elliot's. She threatened to expose your—let me quote the witnesses—'your dirty little secret.'" Beatrice locked eyes with the woman.

"Victoria has been my rival since high school. She dated my husband first. She never got over the fact that he preferred me. She always resented me. Never missed a chance to make some snide comment about my clothing, like she could ever pull off anything as sexy as this." She swept a hand over the body suit.

"So you admit you've known her for some time. Did you also know about her extreme allergy to bee stings?" Sandra asked pointedly.

"Anybody who was around her for more than ten minutes knew about her allergies. Such a drama queen!" Sylvia imitated a high-pitched whine. "Where's my purse? I can't be without my epi pen! Poor me!"

"You and your husband were also at the movie that night. Bradley Jeweler's CCTV shows you both leaving the theater."

"Other people were at that boring film, too. I can't

believe Larry made me go to that pretentious movie. I don't know what he was trying to prove." Her eyes narrowed into a frown. "What are you saying? That someone turned the bees loose on purpose?" She glared at Sandra then Beatrice. "The bees targeted Victoria? That's ridiculous!"

"Is it also ridiculous that you've been seen at Voluptas with Fred Fitzgerald? Is that your dirty little secret?" Sandra's voice rose with the accusation.

"What I do as a consenting adult is none of your business. Get out!" Sylvia slid off her perch and took a menacing step toward Sandra. "You nosy old troublemaker! How dare you accuse me of adultery in my own house!"

Gaston growled deep in his throat and the angry woman froze. "If that dog bites me, I'll sue your ass." She snarled. "It's time for you to leave."

"I have our whole conversation recorded on my cell phone," Sandra said. "I'm sure the officer in charge of the investigation into Victoria's death would be most interested in this discussion."

The display of anger changed to cunning. "You said Victoria's fiancé is paying you to investigate her death. What if I pay double—no triple—what he's paying for you to delete this conversation and forget we ever spoke?"

"That would be unethical," Sandra sputtered. "I could lose my license if I destroyed evidence."

"I didn't kill Victoria. I hated her but I didn't kill her," Sylvia insisted. "I enjoyed making her squirm when she found out I seduced her shining paragon of a father. Why would I do her bodily harm? I was having too much fun pissing her off."

"We have evidence that puts you in the theater the afternoon of the murder." Beatrice shoved the sheaf of papers back into the briefcase and stood up. "And additional information to raise some questions about your relationship with the deceased. You'll be hearing from us again."

"I don't care. Turn your evidence—such as it is—over to the police. It will only prove I'm innocent. I'm calling my lawyer the minute you leave," she hissed. showing them out the door. "So go ahead. Accuse me. You'll be sorry."

The sound of the door slamming reverberated through

the neighborhood. Beatrice put her arm around Sandra's shoulder and gave her a hug. "You were awesome. Just like a real detective. You kept your composure and didn't let Sylvia off the hook. Wait until Detective Johnson hears your recording!"

"Methinks the lady doth protest too much." Sandra said drily.

Chapter Twenty-Seven
Erin on the Case

Friday nights at the movies were always busy, and this Friday was no exception. Erin showed up at work early, hoping to catch Barb alone before the crowds showed up. Unfortunately, Barb was running late. Mark came down to help get the concessions ready. Erin put all the candy out. Mark had the soda machines ready and was just measuring the popcorn and oil when Barb dashed in.

"I'm sorry. My daughter borrowed my car to pick up her kids from school. One of the teachers needed to talk to her about Benjy's grades so she was late." Barb took the measuring cup form Mark. "Thanks. I can take it from here."

A steady stream of customers kept them hopping. A popular musical with some teenage idols was opening so lots of kids bought tickets and loaded up on candy, popcorn, and soda. The line stretched all the way to the front door and never seemed to lighten up. Families lined up for the cartoon feature. Even the middle-aged romance was popular. Erin decided to wait until the movies were well into the last showings. There'd be fewer interruptions. A good time to question Barb about the bad luck at the Classic—get her to blab.

By ten o'clock the line outside concessions finally disappeared. She could hear the rock music booming from the main theater, the squawk of cartoon voices from one of the smaller venues, and faint violins wafting from the other. Barb was cleaning up the popcorn maker. Erin took a deep breath. It was now or never.

"I was just thinking about all the strange things that have been happening here lately." She stopped wiping down the greasy counter and turned to face Barb. "A woman dies in the main theater. Mark told Auntie Sandra the first manager died upstairs. Then I see a spooky looking guy. Do you think it's his ghost?"

"N-n-no!" The older woman stuttered. "Th-there's no ghost in here. Besides, Mark doesn't like us to talk about it. Why scare away customers with crazy rumors?"

"I think it's more than crazy rumors. I get the feeling there's something secret Mark's not telling me." Erin moved between Barb and the popcorn maker. "Auntie Sandra said something about bad luck coming in three's. Did another person die here?"

Barb dropped the cleaning rag into the soapy solution and backed away. "No. No one else died in the Classic, but...."

"But what?" Erin's face lit up as she snapped her fingers. "I knew it. I knew there was another secret, C'mon Barb. Tell me." She moved closer. "I promise not to breathe another word to anyone."

"Mark had an assistant manager a few years ago, right after we got the digital equipment. He hired a techie to help with the transition. Her name was Liz, Liz Lederman. She was kinda mousy, dressed in blouses with Peter Pan collars, frumpy cardigans, and skirts down to her ankles. Out of fashion. But she didn't seem to care."

"Why did Mark hire her?"

"You know what a softie Mark is. She was smart. Really knew her stuff. Got all the digital stuff up and running without a hitch. But she was quiet, kept to herself at first. Didn't look you in the eye when she talked. After a while, she started to warm up to us. Even kidded with Henry, gave him his shit right back. That's why it was so sad when she died."

"Did she die here too?" Erin couldn't keep the excitement out of her voice.

"Nothing like that." Barb spoke in low tones, barely above a whisper. "She committed suicide. Walked off a pier at Madeline Island in Lake Superior. Left a note in her car. But the newspaper kept it hush hush out of respect to her family, said she died unexpectedly. But word gets around. No one guessed she was so depressed."

"So Liz Lederman committed suicide. I understand why Mark avoided the subject. Did she give any reasons?"

"Supposedly she felt trapped in her life. Her sister let it slip she had no friends, been bullied since high school. Kind of a target for harassment by the popular kids. No future in a dead-end job." Barb added hastily, "Her exact words by the way, not mine."

"That's terrible." Erin slowly shook her head. "Mark is so

kind and caring. I can hardly believe she didn't feel appreciated."

"The strange thing is her body was never found. Of course, Lake Superior is the deepest of the Great Lakes. You know how the song goes, *Lake Superior never gives up her dead.* I can't hear those words without thinking about Liz lying at the bottom." She shivered. "It always gives me a chill."

Erin felt the rush of cold, too, just like when the ghost appeared upstairs. She stared into the brightly lit lobby half expecting to see the apparition standing before her. The cell phone in her back pocket vibrated. It was Sandra. *What did you find out?*

Erin stepped into the coat closet before texting back. *Mark hired a woman to help with the transition to digital. Liz Lederman. Committed suicide. Bad Luck no. 3.*

When she returned to concessions, Barb commented, "Important text from your boyfriend?"

"No, nothing like that." Erin sighed. "You know, real life is stranger than the movies, only there's no telling how it will turn out."

Twenty-Eight
You Can't Trust Mondays

On Monday, at exactly one o'clock in the afternoon, Norm and Sandra pulled up to Crawford High School in the battered gray Buick. Erin, with a note from the attendance office in hand, signed herself out at the only unlocked door. She skipped out of the building without so much as a backward glance, hurried to the agreed upon pick up spot far from the school's CCTV cameras and jumped in the back seat.

"What--no Gaston?" she said buckling her seat belt.

"I wanted to bring him, but Norm said no," Sandra complained.

"He's not always dependable," Norm said. "What if he sees a mouse and gives chase? Or gets a bad case of the zoomies? We have one shot at finding the man in the tan suit, and we don't want to blow it."

"You're right." Sandra sighed. "I just feel better when Gaston is around for protection."

"You got me and Uncle Norm today. Don't you think we're enough?"

"Of course I do, Dearie. It's just that he cried so pitifully when we left."

"Two minutes later and he'll be snoozing on the couch." Norm aimed the car toward downtown Crawford. "My appointment with Mark is in fifteen minutes. Let's synchronize our watches."

"This isn't NCIS, Dearie," Sandra said. "Just keep him in his office for fifteen minutes while Erin and I find a spot upstairs to hide, then find a way to get him downstairs while we break into the so-called storeroom."

"How will we do that?" Erin asked.

"No worries, dear girl." Sandra held up a purple crossbody purse with a white poodle stitched on the flap. "I have all my burglary tools right in here. There isn't a locked room or safe that's secure from my breaking and entering skills."

"Wow, Auntie Sandra. Do you think you could teach me how to pick locks?" The girl's eyes gleamed. "I could break into the principal's office and steal any pink behavior slips for after-school detentions. Maybe even charge other kid for my services."

"Stick to the concession stand business. It's a lot safer."

Norm parked the car near the back entrance to the theater.

"I'm going in the front entry. I'll slip to the back and let you in before I go upstairs to Mark's office."

Erin reminded him. "The back door is next to the closet across from the concession stand."

"Got it. Back door near closet. Piece of cake. Mark will be expecting me to come up to his office. Then we move on the second part."

"Do you remember your cover story?" Sandra nodded encouragingly.

"Cover story!" Erin exclaimed. "Wow! Just like *Psych*! I watch that on cable all the time."

"Yeah, I remember." Norm held up his hand and touched each finger as he recited. "First, I say I'm in charge of fund raising for Lend a Paw to Heroes. We're trying to train a service dog for a local vet who's suffering from PTSD."

"Very good. What's next?"

"Second, I tell him we were hoping to show a war movie—like *Saving Private Ryan* on some Tuesday. Third, I ask what Tuesdays are available in November."

"Perfect. Remember to ask lots of questions and talk loudly. Give Erin and me time to get upstairs and hide ourselves before you move on to the next part."

"I got this." Norm gave a thumb's up as he pulled into the back alley and parked. "See ya in five."

Clanking sounds came from the crossbody purse as Sandra slowly made her way down the alley. A huge dumpster, so full the lid would not close, gave off noxious odors, reminding her of the time the garbage disposal sprung a leak. Norm tried his best to fix it, but the leak turned into a waterfall. Good thing she had a plumber on speed dial. She hoped Norm was at the top of his game today.

"Maybe I should carry your purse. I'll tuck it under my arm

so it doesn't make any noise." Erin held out her hand. "We don't want Mark to hear us sneaking up the stairs. And watch where I put my feet. I know which step is creaky."

Erin slipped the purse over her shoulder and tucked it tightly under her arm. "Gosh, this thing is heavy."

"Comes with the detective territory. I don't even have my revolver yet. I need to take the concealed carry course first."

The back door swung outward. Norm held it open while the two of them passed by, then he closed it so slowly there was barely a sound as the door shut tightly. Sandra returned his thumbs up, and he scurried back to the main lobby. They waited in the back hall listening to his footsteps thundering up the steps. A loud "Hello, are you Mark? I'm Norm Clodfelder. I called you earlier about a possible fundraiser for my group."

When they heard the door to Mark's office slam shut, Erin tiptoed over to the staircase. She pointed to the third step up, and put a finger to her lips. Then she cautiously tread on the first two steps, without making a sound. Sandra did her best to follow. They could hear Norm rattling off the names of all the members of his group, while Mark commented, ''Wow. I didn't realize there were that many veterans in Crawford."

When they reached the top of the stairs, Erin pointed to a large box and gestured for Sandra to sit on it. After quietly pushing aside the cardboard cut-outs blocking the storeroom door, the girl crouched down behind Chewbacca.

Thankfully they didn't have long to wait. Norm vigorously pumped Mark's hand in the doorway, and said, "I'll get back to ya about those dates once I check with the guys. We really appreciate your help."

"I'll walk you down the stairs." Mark stepped into the hallway.

"Nah, I can find my way out. It was good doing business with ya." Norm gave him a wave and started down the hall, without a glance toward Chewbacca and the hidden detectives.

Sandra stared at Erin with her hands folded near her heart and her head down, listening intently for Norm's next move. Blood pounded through her skull with the thumping of her heart. Erin knelt behind the cut-out with fingers crossed, scarcely making a sound as she slowly inhaled and exhaled. It was only a few heartbeats but it seemed like an eternity until they heard Norm shout up the stairs.

"Mark! Mark! I need your help. I just took a dump and the toilet is overflowing. I need a plunger real bad."

Mark yelled, "Be right there." He rushed out of his office, leaving the door ajar. A rectangle of bright light illuminated the dim hallway, as Norm continued his litany. "I'm sorry, man. It's a big mess down here. Like a volcano erupted. And the handle is stuck. Keeps on flushing."

The harried manager thundered past them, cursing under his breath, "Not again! Goddam old plumbing. Another shit storm! Just what I need today!"

After his footsteps on the stairs faded away, Sandra slowly rose up from the box. She glided next to Erin and reached for her purse. The elderly woman pulled out a flashlight, handing it to the girl as she rummaged for her pick and wrench. Before she got started on the lock, Erin turned the doorknob and the door swung open. She shone the light into the room and hesitated before stepping inside. Sandra followed closely behind her. A musty smell of mouse droppings and moldy air assaulted her nostrils. No stacks of boxes and old posters blocked their way.

Instead she saw a metal table with tarnished chrome legs when she turned her phone's flashlight onto the room. Through the thin veneer of dirt, she could make out the speckled red top, similar to a table she once owned. She swept the light across the room. Two matching metal tubular chairs with red padded backs bookended the table. One had a large tear with stuffing hanging out. In the corner stood a small, once white refrigerator with a rounded top and a silver Coldspot emblem. No oven, just a two-burner hot plate with a frayed fabric-covered cord.

"This is no storeroom," Sandra exclaimed. "It's like a time travel into the past."

Erin's beam settled on an old photograph hanging on the wall. The bearded man frowned balefully at them. His sinister eyes seemed to track their movements as they crept farther into the room. "And it's creepy as hell," she whispered.

She shifted her light to the floor. The thick layer of dust had been recently disturbed. A pattern of shoeprints led from the outer door to the table and beyond to the next room. Sandra sneezed and the sound seemed to echo through the building. The startled girl almost dropped her light as she squealed. "Yikes!"

"It's all right, Dearie. Mark can't hear anything with Norm talking at him," Sandra reassured her.

"Someone has been in here." The girl pointed to the footprints that disappeared behind the closed door and gulped. "The man in the tan suit."

A thin beam of sunlight wavered through a tear in the drawn shades of the front window, exposing an intricate cobweb that stretched from windowsill to curtain rod. The decayed shells of several stink bugs dangled from the fine threads. Sandra felt another sneeze coming on, but grasped her nose with her free hand to stifle it.

Erin raised her light to the closed door of the next room and shivered. "Should we check what's behind that door?"

Sandra took a cautious step toward the dark foreboding door, but froze when she heard a scuttling sound. Erin whimpered, "I don't like it here. What if there's rats?' She ran the flashlight beam along the floorboards, pausing on the cracks in the woodwork. "I think I saw something move!"

"The man in the tan suit must have been thirsty,' Sandra said. She spotlighted a can of Coke Zero on a small end table next to the door.

"Did they have Coke Zero back in the sixties?" Erin asked. She added her light to Sandra's. The silver and red metal gleamed in their combined rays.

"No. Our ghost must have a modern-day pal," Sandra muttered, as she slowly explored every inch of the table with her light.

"Stop there!" Erin said. The girl firmly grasped her arm to keep it from moving. Sandra's flashlight illuminated a small brown box, rectangular in shape with a mesh covering. "Look. It's another bee cage." She let go of Sandra's arm to reach for the box.

"No, don't touch it." Sandra placed her free arm in front of the girl. "It's evidence. We want the police to find it. We just have to convince them Victoria's death was no accident. The bee cage is proof someone premeditated her murder."

She began to take pictures of the Coke can and brown box with her phone. "I'm going to show these photos to that police detective. He can't claim I'm a crazy old lady when he sees this."

"Let's get out of here," Erin's voice trembled with a sense of urgency. "We don't know how long Uncle Norm can keep Mark in the men's room."

"Don't worry, Dearie. I'm sure he has the shituation under control."

Chapter Twenty-Nine
Deja View

Mark's frustrated voice boiled over from the men's room. Norm offered advice, like "Maybe lift the whatchamacallit." And "Do ya got a wet vac somewhere?" The suggestions weren't very helpful to the fuming manager, as far as Sandra could tell. The f-bomb exploded several times from his mouth.

She and Erin scurried along the dim hallway. Erin offered the elderly sleuth her arm at the top of the stairs. Sandra gratefully held on. The adrenalin flowing made her hands shaky and her feet unsteady. A fall would be disastrous; explaining their presence in the empty theater to the already seething manager could end Erin's career in food service, plus place a back mark on their fledgling detective business.

Sandra clung tightly to the teenager as they cleared the concession stand and the coat closet. When she stumbled on the uneven floor in the old theater, Erin shifted her body closer for more stability. After the back door firmly closed behind them, Sandra finally let a loud exhale, dropping her hands to her sides and willing her body to stop shaking.

"I'm glad to be safely outside! What a nerve-wracking day!"

Erin danced in the alley, swinging the clanging crossbody purse from side to side. "We did it! We found more evidence! Now the cops will have to believe us. I can't wait to tell Dad and Beatrice."

"Hold on a minute. For now, this has to be our secret! Your dad may not agree that the end justifies the means. He won't like you skipping school to do some sleuthing. Your mother will blow a gasket if she finds out. We're going to stick to our story for the school. I needed you along for a doctor's appointment because Norm had a conflict."

"What about the soda can and bee cage?"

"I'm going to show the team what was in the storeroom.

I'm just leaving you out of it. I'll say I snuck in while Norm kept Mark busy."

"Isn't that lying?"

"It's more like fibbing. Just a little white lie of omission."

As they sat in the car waiting for Norm, Sandra showed Erin the photos she had taken. The dim light in the abandoned room made the bee cage hard to see. Erin asked for the phone. "I can edit the picture in Photos. I'll play with the lighting. See if I can get a better resolution." She adjusted the exposure and brilliance. The image of the bee cage became much clearer.

When the girl held up the improved visual for her to see, Sandra said, "Excellent job, Sweetie! See if you can work your magic on the Coke can."

Erin was still editing the picture when Norm appeared.

"Whadda ya doing there?" he asked.

"I'm improving the pictures of the evidence we just found," Erin said as Sandra gave him a brief rundown of what they found in the long-dead manager's old apartment. "We think the killer used it as a hide out. We saw footprints that no ghost left behind."

"What about yer footprints? Didn't ya walk in the dust too? If the culprit comes back, won't he know somebody's been there? He'll see different shoe prints from his."

"Damn, I didn't think of that. Hopefully ours will blend in with the tracks already there." She glanced at Erin in the back seat, engrossed in her task with the cell phone. "Let's get Erin back to school and head directly to the police station from there.

***

The police station felt like a sepulcher, sterile and cold. "Sorry. Detective Johnson's not here. He's out on a shoplifting call." The same young, uniformed man was at the desk, tapping keys on a bulky desktop computer. He paused as Sandra watched. "Would you like to make an appointment to talk to him?"

"Yes. We'd like to see him today if possible." She waved her cell phone at the young man. "There's been some new developments in the case we're investigating. He'll be very interested in what we've discovered."

'I have no clue how long he'll be at the $uperSaver. There's a shoplifting ring from Chicago hitting small towns across the state border. He's finally caught a break in the case." The policeman checked his computer. "It looks like he has some time tomorrow at ten. Should I put you on his schedule?"

"Of course. My name is Sandra Tooksbury. I'll be here tomorrow at ten sharp."

***

Later that night, Vlad gave a long whistle when he saw the bee cage in the photo. "You took this picture in the supposed storeroom?"

Sandra nodded, "Norm kept Mark busy while I snooped around. That apartment looked just like the manager left it when he died fifty years ago. It was like walking into a mausoleum until we saw the footprints, the bee cage, and the Coke can. Signs of the living, not the dead."

"Who would have access to the storeroom?" Vlad wondered aloud.

"The people that work there, mainly. Unless the killer had previous ties to the Classic and remembered the room upstairs. Larry Treptow maybe worked there when he was in high school. He married into money, didn't come from it himself."

"You did some first-rate detective work." Beatrice said. "That obstinate cop can't deny evidence right before his eyes."

"I should hope not." Sandra said with a grave expression on her face. "We'll find out tomorrow."

***

Sandra sat across from the detective in the same uncomfortable chair as before with piles of papers at her feet. When she set her cell phone on the desk before Detective Johnson, skepticism was written all over his face. "What do you have to show me?"

"There were several suspects at the movie that afternoon— all caught coming out of the Classic on CCTV camera." She showed him some stills of the footage featuring the waiter, Larry and Sylvia Treptow. "Some have a history of run-ins with the deceased. Larry Treptow lost his promotion when Victoria returned."

"Doesn't make him a killer," Johnson snorted.

"The dark-haired woman in the long coat is his wife, Sylvia. She had a heated altercation at the restaurant where the young man in the picture worked. In fact, I have her on audio trying to bribe me into dropping our investigation. Would you like to hear it?"

"I suppose," he said with a sigh of resignation. His frown deepened as he listened to Sylvia's vituperative voice. "O.K. There's bad blood between the two women. A cat fight doesn't necessarily lead to murder."

"How about this? Physical evidence that the bee attack was premeditated." Sandra showed him the photos of the soft drink can and bee cage. "We found these in the storeroom at the theater."

"What the hell? A Coke can and a little wooden box are proof that Victoria Fitzgerald was murdered?"

"The wooden box is a cage for transporting bees. We found one earlier in the theater where Victoria died. I showed it to you, begged you to test it for fingerprints, but you tossed me out of your office." Her eyes blazed with indignation.

His face flushed a dull red. "I know. I thought it was an open and shut case. An accidental death due to anaphylactic shock. You're telling me I might have made an error in judgement."

"I shouldn't have to do your job for you," she snapped.

"How did you happen to come by this fresh evidence you're showing me?"

Now it was Sandra's turn to blush. "I broke into the storeroom while my colleague distracted Mark, the owner."

"Why didn't you just ask Mark if you could take a look around?" He raised a quizzical eyebrow.

"Mark is in a big state of denial about all the tragic events that have been happening at the Classic, going way back to when Oscar O'Brian was discovered dead in the upstairs apartment. I guess people dying in your theater is bad for business."

"He's not going to be any happier when the cops show up," Detective Johnson noted wryly.

"Mark seems like a good person. He'll want to know the truth."

"Someone stole Victoria's epi pen, brought some bees in a so-called cage and trained them to kill her; I still find this all pretty far-fetched." Johnson's mouth twisted into a cynical scowl.

Sandra felt anger pull her upright. "You're insinuating I'm a kook. That I made this all up. Meanwhile a killer is out on the streets."

The detective thrust his hands up, waving them to placate her. "Easy, Mrs. Tooksbury. Easy. I'm not accusing you of manufacturing evidence. I'll get a warrant to search the theater. We'll check out the old apartment, Dust the objects for fingerprints, including the ones you brought in earlier. See if we can find a distinguishing tread on the shoes. Of course, I'll have to check out the soles of the shoes you were wearing, as well."

Sandra squeezed her eyes shut for a minute and shook her head. When she opened them, she said in a sheepish tone. "You'll have to check my niece's shoes too. She also walked into the room."

Johnson rolled his eyes. "I'm not even going to ask. Bring in everything you got. Come in tomorrow with the girl and wear the same shoes. We'll take your prints. Now please get out and let me get back to work."

Chapter Thirty
Promising Developments

"What the hell were you thinking?" Vlad spat. His stormy eyes were fixed on Sandra's downcast face. He barely suppressed the rage in his voice as he lashed out at Erin and Sandra. Even Gaston could feel Vlad's anger being unleashed. He sheepishly covered his head with his paws.

Red-faced, Vlad's shouting continued. "I've come to expect reckless behavior from you. You're a grown woman. You recognize the consequences, however risky. It's part of the investigation. But to include my innocent and trusting daughter with your hare-brained schemes… and to forge an excuse for her absence! You've absolutely gone too far."

He stood in the over-heated living room, fists on hips. His daughter and Sandra were seated side by side on the chintz covered love seat, with the little poodle cowering between them. Whether the warmth came from his anger, or a raised thermostat was impossible to determine.

Finally Erin spoke. "But Dad, I was going to explore the storeroom on my own. Auntie Sandra went along to protect me." The girl placed a hand over the elderly woman's which were folded meekly in her lap. Gaston gave her fingers a lick.

"I realize your pre-frontal lobe is still developing and teenagers struggle with impulse control. But skipping school to sneak into an empty theater crosses all boundaries. Plus it could have been dangerous. What if the killer was hiding out there and you stumbled into him?"

The intensity of her father's glare made Erin shrink inside. She could count on one hand the number of times her father got angry, and never like this, never at her. She bit her lip and studied her feet, reluctant to meet his gaze.

"Worse is how I found out about your shenanigans," Vlad sputtered as he stalked in front of the love seat. "I get a call from Detective Johnson asking me to bring you down to the station to check your shoes for prints. When I ask what for, he tells me about you breaking into the abandoned apartment. And then they take your fingerprints as well, like you're a suspect."

"They had to rule us out so forensics could focus on the other footprints in the dust." Sandra gently reminded him. "You know how these investigations work."

Vlad stopped his pacing and glowered at his daughter. "I only know my sixteen-year-old daughter is now part of a murder investigation. And you're very lucky the police called me and not your mother. I had to beg that bellicose bully not to include your statement in his report because of your tender age."

"I am so grateful you stood up for me, Dad." Erin walked over and threw her arms around his rigid shoulders. "We did find evidence. Now the police are getting a search warrant. Isn't that a positive development for the case?"

Gaston yipped and ran in a circle around the father and daughter. He stopped at Vlad's feet and tugged gently at his pant's cuff, wagging his tail.

"I'm sorry. I made a mistake. Erin's off the case. She won't be involved any more. Gaston is trying to tell you to stop being so angry," Sandra said. "Punish Erin if you must, but let's not tell Maria." The pooch drifted back to her side.

Vlad held his daughter at arm's length as he spoke. "You are grounded from your phone for a week. You're leaving it in my car. Tell your mom you forgot it."

Erin nodded, resigned to losing her cell phone and her nightly chats with her friends. "O.K. Dad. I'm sorry. I was wrong."

Vlad leveled a piercing stare at Sandra. "And YOU! You are not to hijack my daughter on any more trespassing expeditions."

"I promise to keep Erin out of any more sleuthing. From now on, it's just Gaston and me."

***

The police visit to the Classic Cinema didn't make front page headlines in the Daily Gazette, but the whole town of Crawford was abuzz with speculation about why the cops would have a search warrant for the second-floor storeroom. Even at Crawford High School, rumors were flying. Walking down the hall the next day, Erin heard kids talking in excited voices.

"I heard the cops found a decomposed body like one of those bog bodies they found in Ireland. Nothing but gobs of hair, black skin over bones."

"My dad said maybe they had a fentanyl shipment hidden up there. Lots of people go in and out of the Classic. It's be a great place for dealing drugs."

"Maybe the manager was growing marijuana up there with Grow Lights. He looks kinda like an old hippie."

Erin ducked her head into her half open locker as a group of gossip mongers drew near. She'd purposely worn a Crawford High sweatshirt and distressed blue jeans to blend in with the other kids. After a before school conference with the principal and her father, she plodded through her morning classes, slouching silently in the back of each room, scarcely daring to raise her hand.

"Hey Erin? Don't you work at the Classic? We've seen you there." A perky red head with long wavy hair and a short skirt stopped to chat.

Erin bent farther down and flipped through a stack of notebooks at the bottom of her locker. "Just a second," she answered from inside her locker. "I can't find my geometry folder." She fumbled some more with the folders. "Oh, here it is." She straightened up, hoping the girls had given up and left. No such luck. "What were you saying?"

"I asked you about the movie theater. Why were the cops searching the place?" The group of girls listened intently for her answer.

"I'm just a kid. I have no idea what's going on. I don't go in until tomorrow night. If I find out anything, I'll let you know." She made a clueless expression, and hurried away.

That night, Erin found herself the center of more unwanted attention from her mother. She was lying in her bed, reading *The Great Gatsby* for English, when Maria peered in her room. "Can you please give me a hand with supper?"

"Sure, Mom." Instead of protesting and complaining, Erin's immediately put down he book, patiently following her mother into the kitchen. Maria didn't notice the blip on the radar screen of unusual teen behavior; she handed the girl some apples, pears, bananas, and a small knife. "Can you throw together a fruit salad while I check the chicken casserole in the crock pot?"

Maria lifted the glass cover and stirred the fragrant contents. She turned to Erin, and watched her cut fruit on the chopping board for a moment. Then she strolled to the family room to make sure the younger children were engaged with something on the Disney channel before she cleared her throat and quietly spoke.

"Alice—the lady from church who works at the drug store right next door—told me a squad car full of cops pulled up in front of the Classic Cinema on Tuesday. They were in there for hours. They came out with some bags. They must have found something, but the cops are being pretty tight lipped." Her mother looked at her suspiciously. "Do you know anything about that?"

Erin looked up from her chore, wearing her best poker face. "No, Mom. I was in school all day. I haven't a clue."

Maria continued in a harsh tone, "If there's something illegal going on, I don't want you working there. In fact, I forbid it."

Erin set the knife down and turned toward her mother. "Every kid in town goes to movies there with their parents. Do you think all those people would show up if they thought a crime was being committed? This is Crawford. The biggest crime is not picking up after your dog poops in the park."

"I suppose you're right," Maria said reluctantly She leaned closer, concern written all over her face. "Ever since that Fitzgerald woman died, you've been too quiet. Seeing a dead person for the first time is quite a shock. It's bound to cause some distress, maybe even nightmares. Please be honest with me. Are you feeling anxious or depressed?"

"No Mom. I'm fine. I talked to Dad about it. He gave me some good advice." *Including keeping you in the dark about snooping in the storeroom.*

"Hah! Your Dad should take some of his own advice. He's a changed man since he found that woman dead in the bookstore, and not for the better. It's that crazy old lady and her dog. I hope she's not bamboozling you, too." Her mother frowned from forehead to chin.

"Auntie Sandra is so kind and loving. You got her all wrong." Erin said earnestly.

"Maybe I should make an appointment for you with the

school psychologist. You should talk to a professional." She looked at the dry erase calendar on the bulletin board and picked up the attached pen. "I'll call the high school tomorrow," she said as she scribbled a note on a square.

"If it will make you happy, I'll talk to someone." Erin didn't want to burst her mom's bubble, but appointments with the school psychologist were months in the making.

One psychologist for fifteen hundred students. I'm safe from any shrink's meddling.

"I don't think you should go into work tomorrow night. I don't trust that manager."

"Mom, haven't you heard someone's presumed innocent until proven guilty? Mark's a really good guy. He'd never do anything wrong. Look at all he does for charities. Please let me go to work tomorrow. Please," Erin begged.

Her mother shook her finger at the girl. "If there's the slightest hint of trouble, you are to call me immediately and I'll come and get you. Promise?"

"I promise."

Chapter Thirty-One
Writing on the Wall

Please come to work early. Mark's text signaled to Erin all was not well at the Classic Cinema. When she arrived at concessions, Barb was sitting on her tall stool, elbow on knee, chin in hand, looking like her favorite aunt had just died. The concession stand was as quiet as the principal's office when he asked who wrote *School sucks* in lipstick on the girl's bathroom mirror.

"You're finally here," the older woman said, her voice cracking. "Mark wants us to meet upstairs in his office. Bad news!"

Erin widened her eyes in a good imitation of an innocent bystander. "What's up?"

"The cops were here yesterday. They found something in the old storeroom but wouldn't let on what. Every nosy Parker in town showed up last night, but none of them stayed to watch a movie. This morning we had to go to the police station and get fingerprinted—even do a swab for a DNA sample. Just like we were the criminals."

Mark interrupted their conversation with a shout from the top of the stairs, "Is Erin here? I'd like to start our meeting."

"I just got here, Mark. Let me hang up my coat." Erin scurried to the closet.

"Coming up, Boss," Barb called back. She trudged up the stairs with all the enthusiasm of a turncoat about to face a firing squad. Erin found maintaining her façade of innocence becoming harder.

Two empty folding chairs awaited them in the office. They carefully threaded their way past a pile of posters and sat down. Henry was slouched on a rickety wood chair scraping dirt from beneath his fingernails. He grunted a greeting at his co-workers and resumed studying his hands.

Mark slumped in his swivel chair, elbows resting on the armrests. His red-rimmed eyes betrayed a lack of sleep. The last time Erin had seen such a sad expression on a man's face was when her dad told them he was moving out. She felt the same knot of pain in the pit of her stomach as her boss started to speak.

He bravely tried to smile before but failed miserably. "I asked you to come early today to let you know what happened yesterday when the police came in with a search warrant to examine the storeroom on the second floor. The detective in charge asked me to come down to the station and get fingerprinted. He also asked all of you to do the same."

"He made us do a DNA swab, too. What the hell was that all about?" Henry grumbled.

"Are they going to shut the theater down?' Barb asked fearfully. "I heard they found illegal drugs."

"I've heard all kinds of crazy rumors too. I want to share what I just learned from the head cop, Detective Johnson. Some of it good news, some of it bad."

"Do they think one of us is a pusher?' Barb asked fearfully. "Did they find illegal drugs in the storeroom?"

"Nothing like that. All the big cop would say is that's it's part of an ongoing murder investigation. He wanted to rule out Classic employees."

"Murder? Is there a killer on the loose?" Barb blurted out.

"You mean Victoria Fitzgerald! That bitch can ruin lives from beyond the grave," Henry exploded. "Too bad it wasn't her old man that died."

Erin was shocked at the projectionist's display of anger. Barb's mouth dropped open in surprise and even Mark leaned back from the man's bitter expression.

When he found his voice, Mark said, "Please don't speak ill of the dead. Yes, it's because of Victoria. It seems there's been an intruder in the storeroom. The door was unlocked. Even I saw some footprints in the dust. Have any of you gone in there recently?" He stared at each of them.

"No way," Henry grumbled. "Why the hell would anybody want to go in that old room? It's been locked ever since I started working here twenty some years ago."

"I don't even like going up those stairs with my bad knees." Barb said. "Much less moving all that junk aside to get into a dusty room.'

Mark's gaze settled on Erin. She tried not to squirm. "Ever since I saw the man in the tan suit, I avoid the second floor. I don't want to see that creepy ghost again."

"That's what I told the police. But they still wanted us all to be fingerprinted and get swabbed."

"No problem," Barb said. "Anything to get past this nightmare."

"Just like the cops to stir up trouble," Henry sneered.

"I'll go tomorrow after school." Erin crossed her fingers. Was this a lie of omission? She neglected to tell them her dad already took her to the police station with Auntie Sandra for shoe and fingerprints.

"That's the good news. We're being cleared of suspicion."

"Hah," Henry interrupted.

"The bad news is our customers may be scared away. If business doesn't pick up, we're doomed. So the sooner the police catch the killer, the better. So let's all co-operate and do our best to act like everything is normal." Mark's eyes lingered on Henry, but the projectionist stared blankly ahead.

Mark rubbed his hands together as he spoke. "If we keep a positive attitude, our patrons will pick up on our vibes. Agreed?"

Barb and Erin nodded in agreement.

"Great!" The manager clasped his hands overhead like a winning prize fighter. "Only one showing on Thursdays. Our short day. Now let's get to work."

***

Movie goers trickled in. Most came out of curiosity and tried to pump Erin and Barb for information. "Is it true the cops were here yesterday? What's going on?"

"There's a lot of rumors floating around about the police visit. Mark wouldn't be in trouble, would he?"

"My kid came home from high school with a crazy story about a drug bust. What's up with that?"

"I heard the cops found another person dead in the old upstairs apartment."

And on and on until the movies started.

Barb fielded all the questions while selling tickets and filling bags with popcorn. "There's never been any drugs on the premises. Mark's fine. He's working tonight. The police said it's part of an ongoing investigation. They will release their findings when all the information is in. The theater is not in trouble. Enjoy the movie."

Erin handed out candy and soft drinks, moving robotically from task to task, shrugging her shoulders when pressed for information. "Everything's fine as far as I know. I'm just a kid."

The credits were running in the big theater, the last show to run. Barb collapsed on the stool, arms dangling at her side. Deep lines made a road map on her tired face. She pushed straggly hair off her perspiring brow.

"What a night!" Every word seemed to take superhuman effort from the older lady. "Please be a sweetheart and pick up the trash under the seats. Mark will haul out the vacuum when everyone's gone."

"Sure thing." Erin said, eager to step away from the concessions for a minute. Faking ignorance was exhausting. She couldn't forget for one second how important solving the case was for Auntie Sandra and Gaston. Most of all for her dad.

Maybe Mom will get off his back if they figure out who killed Victoria.

The last moviegoers strolled past her in the lobby. For once, she was glad to walk down the deserted hallway by herself, free from prying eyes and nosy questions. The lights flickered nervously as she strode past the familiar movie lines. Perusing the quotes was like reading a favorite storybook from her childhood.

"ET phone home."
"There's no crying in baseball."
"Frankly, my dear, I don't give a damn."
"I'm gonna make him an offer he can't refuse."

All were old friends by now, comforting her along the shadow-filled journey to the oldest theater. The twitching of the lights triggered a matching current throughout her body. "I've got nerves that jingle, jangle, jingle." She hummed the tune from an old movie to soothe herself.

When is Mark going to get the damn lights fixed? This a lawsuit waiting to happen.

One foot placed cautiously in front of the other, not wanting to trip, she took longer than usual. She hoped her dad didn't grow too impatient waiting for her in the car. *No sense pissing him off more than I have already.*

Erin had almost reached the last quote over the door to the empty theater. *It's a trap* and of course the disclaimer warning of the drop down. *NO. Really. Watch your step.*

Then she noticed the red paint dripping down the wall, like drizzles down a window during a heavy rain. The long streaks bled into each other, making the words below hard to read.

Mark must have been in a hurry. The new quote's a pretty sloppy job.

Erin slowed to a stop and squinted at the recent addition—so recent the paint was still wet in spots. Her heart thumped wildly when she recognized her name. Her chest tightened like iron bands were squeezing the breath—no the life—out of her. Then a lump grew to boulder size in her throat as she deciphered the words.

So deep red they could have been written in blood.

ERIN CHOMSKY

GET OUT WHILE YOU CAN

Chapter Thirty-Two
The Mane Action

The last person Sandra expected to call her the next day was Detective Johnson. She had a standing appointment every Thursday night at her favorite beauty salon, Curl Up and Dye. Chrissy, her stylist, had just started washing her hair after coloring it "Starlit Red." Sandra laid back, head resting on the sink, and admired the fleur de lis design of the vintage tin panels in the remodeled salon. Chrissy's salon kept the original charm of the old downtown building with its exposed brick walls and ornate ceiling. Soon the stylist was treating her to a head massage so relaxing she let out a soft moan,

That moment of shear ecstasy was interrupted by the shrill ring tone of her phone. Sandra intended to ignore it, but Gaston started barking and wouldn't stop.

Chrissy allowed her long-time customers to bring their well-behaved pooches into her shop. She even called Gaston her "little Shampoodle." Sometimes Sandra entertained the fellow customers with his show biz antics, but not today. The poodle's behavior was anything but charming. Chrissy frowned at the commotion and stopped her gentle rubs. The other stylist and her customer shot him dirty looks.

"Oh, dear. It seems I must take this call," Sandra said.

"No worries," Chrissy said as she wrapped a towel around her dripping head. "There's plenty more clean towels where this one came from."

Gaston ceased barking the minute she clicked on the green phone icon and said a tentative "Hello."

"Mrs. Tooksbury?" a gruff voice said. "This is Detective Randy Johnson. Are you available to take a call?"

The soggy towel had already muffled the sound of his voice, so Sandra could barely make out what the man was saying. "Who did you say you were?"

When he repeated his name louder, three pairs of eyes

turned to stare at her. The pleasant murmur of the ladies' voices turned to complete silence, as they leaned closer to eavesdrop on her conversation.

"Just a minute," Sandra said, "Let me step away into a quieter room." The only quieter spot with any privacy was the restroom. Sandra scurried into the lavatory, Gaston at her side, and closed the door. Luckily the fragrance of Vanilla Bean masked the unpleasant odor of flatulence that lingered from the previous inhabitant.

"How can I be of assistance?" she asked in her most professional voice,

"I wanted you to know we found the evidence, just like in your photos. We ran all the fingerprints of the Class Cinema's staff as well as the waiter from Elliot's Inn. There was no match to the ones on the soda can and bee cages. We also asked for a swab to see if there was a DNA match. Nothing there either. We have an unknown assailant so far."

"Nothing on the purse or the letter?'

"Only the victim's and an unknown set."

"What about Larry and Sylvia Treptow? Anything there?"

"They declined to come in. Their lawyer said attending the same movie doesn't establish guilt. Our investigation has stalled until we can convince them it's in their best interest to clear their names."

Unless one of them is guilty, she thought, but didn't say it aloud. "What's next? Are you going to have a press conference?"

"Tim from the Daily Gazette stopped by, but we have nothing concrete that we can state at this time."

"So we're done."

"No, *you're* done. We have a couple of leads we're checking out. As a courtesy to your dogged determination, no pun intended, I've apprised you of the current situation. But now I want you to back off. Stand down and let us do our job."

Gaston let out a sharp yip and put his front paws above Sandra's knee.

As if he were addressing the poodle, the detective said, "And don't depend on your dog to keep you safe. Wait for our investigators to handle the case."

Sandra dragged herself back to the shampoo area and slid

back into the reclining chair. Gaston stood sentinel by the outer door quietly waiting for the hairdresser to finish. Chrissy rinsed the shampoo out of her hair and applied some conditioner with the scent of lilacs. After a vigorous towel drying, the stylist asked, "Your call wouldn't have anything to do with the police raid on the Classic Cinema?"

"Chrissy, even if I knew, I wouldn't be at liberty to divulge any information. I could be charged with obstruction." Sandra moved to the chair with the large mirror and viewed her hair color approvingly. Chrissy began trimming some of her locks, then got out the blow dryer.

"Alice from the drug store said it's a murder investigation—probably that Fitzgerald woman. The coroner ruled it accidental because of bee stings but I thought it could be a poison dart, like on that Midsomer Murders episode," said the woman getting her hair rolled in little slips of foil. "The killer used a blow gun he'd brought back from Africa. Staged it near a beehive."

"You know, I never did trust that manager, Mark Whathisname. He always acts so nice. Nobody can be that nice all the time," her stylist said.

"Remember that woman who committed suicide? The one that just started working there?" the foil head asked.

"Yeah, Liz Ledbetter. I went to high school with her. Victoria and the popular girls never got along with her. She was a big brainiac. Kind of a nerd," the young hairdresser added.

"Her death was suspicious too. I heard she'd been bullied. It could have been the manager bullying her," the customer suggested.

"And her body was never found. Maybe she didn't drown in Lake Superior. She could be walled up somewhere in the Classic." The stylist excitedly dropped her comb with this revelation. "She's probably a skeleton by now."

"I personally know Mark Hoffman," Sandra spoke up. "He would never harm anyone. A kinder, more generous man never lived. I can't listen to you bad mouth him anymore. Can we please change the topic of conversation?"

"Yes, please," said Chrissy. "If you can't say anything good…You know how rumors spread in this town. Let's check the facts before we talk about people." With a can of Super Hold spray, she put the finishing touches on Sandra's hairdo.

"Here's a fact. I saw Kent Jacobs driving Ramona Runde home after pickleball. They were parked in front of her house for a long time and they weren't just talking," said the customer.

"OOH! I can't wait 'til Deb finds out." The stylist squealed. "She'll be so pissed."

Sandra handed Chrissy her credit card and sighed, thinking. *Only a fool thinks tearing someone else down builds you up.*

Gaston stood by the door as far away from the chatter as he could get. When he saw Sandra close her purse and walk toward him, he began whimpering and picked up the handle of his leash, trotting toward her, leash in mouth. She bent down to and grasped the soggy leather. "You're certainly in a hurry to get home."

She peered out the salon front window and saw that Norm had parked the Buick in front. "Let's go. Uncle Norm is here."

As she opened the door, the dog yanked on the leash, barking frantically. Sandra noted the coffee shop was a few blocks down the street. "No, Lovey Puppy. We're not going for treats today."

She juggled holding onto her purse with the dog straining against the leash. Gaston flung his whole body down the stoop in front of the salon, forcing Sandra off balance. As she struggled to right herself, her purse spilled on the concrete and the pooch broke free. He tore down the street as fast as his four little legs could move, dragging the leash behind him.

"Damn you, Gaston," Sandra shouted as she surveyed the scattered contents with dismay. "No treats for YOU!"

Norm rushed to her side and whistled, "You look tressed to kill." He bent down and began shoving items back into her bag. "Let me get that for you," he said. His ponytail bobbed from the back of the Green Bay Packer cap as he reached for a lipstick the had rolled down the step. Sandra loomed above him, hands on hips. If looks could kill, Gaston would be lying on his back in the street, four paws in the air.

"I'm so mad at that darn dog. He nearly knocked me for a loop. I could've fallen and broken something," she said as Norm handed her the purse. "He'll do anything for a Puppuccino from Literatus."

"I guess I better chase after him," Norm said. "If someone

opens the door to the coffee shop, he'll scoot in and cause trouble." Norm helped Sandra down the steps. "You wait here."

A little boy with his grandmother was pointing at the display of children's books in the window of the combination coffee shop and bookstore. Gaston barreled down the sidewalk in their direction. His yips could be heard from blocks away.

The older lady swept the child up in her arms as the dog sped past. "Watch out, you naughty dog!"

Gaston raced down Main Street like he was being pursued by a mob of zombie dog catchers.

"What the hell!" exclaimed Norm. "He's heading for the movie theater."

"Oh dear! Erin's working today," Sandra cried "Hurry! Get in the car. Something must be wrong."

Chapter Thirty-Three
Not the Fall that Hurts

Erin pivoted and ran down the shadowy hall. She remembered what her mother last said: "If there's the slightest hint of trouble, you are to call me immediately and I'll come and get you." The writing on the wall contained much more than a hint of trouble. It was an out and out scream.

Her phone was in her jacket pocket in the closet. She slowed down when she got to the concession stand and called out. "Barb! Come and see what's on the wall!"

No Barb. Erin leaned over the counter to check if she was picking up trash from the floor. Nope. She must be out in the alley having a smoke. Erin scurried past concessions and opened the closet door. Barb's coat was gone. But the familiar smell of cigarette smoke that clung to her clothes lingered.

Erin slipped on her jacket, reaching into the pocket. The cool comforting feel of her cell phone reassured her that help was only a phone call away.

The girl pressed the side button to turn it on. Her hand trembled as she swept her thumb across the screen and paused above the green phone icon. Before she called Mom, she probably should tell Mark she was leaving and why. She wanted to see the expression on his face when she told him about the red paint on the wall. If he didn't do it, then who did?

Thrusting the phone and her hand back into her pocket, she crossed over to the stairs leading up to the second floor. Mark was probably finishing up, tallying the tickets sold that night and matching it to the amount of money. God knows what Henry would be doing? Probably looking at some reels on his phone, or posting something stupid on Facebook or X or whatever lame site he followed. Ever since the newspaper clipping incident, she swore he gave her snake eyes whenever he saw her, even though she had nothing to do with the long-ago death of his sister.

Once I call Mom, my theater gig is over, She'll never let me come back. Erin felt like a rat abandoning ship. But someone clearly wanted her out of the picture. *I'm not about to argue with a killer.*

She slowly walked up the stairs for the last time, avoiding the tear in the carpet. But she stomped on the squeaky step as hard as she could. No one was around to hear the racket.

Erin froze at the top of the stairs. The upstairs hall was eerily quiet. Normally Mark and Henry would be yakking away as they finished for the night, arguing about who was going to clean the men's room. No voices.

The path to the office was no longer an obstacle course. The mannequin's legs were in an upright position, a disembodied figure waiting for its top half. Boxes were shoved against the wall. The empty reels were stacked neatly into a tower, instead of lying scattered. Chewbacca still guarded the storeroom entrance with the door left ajar. Mark must have cleaned up after the police search.

"Mark? Are you up here?" Erin called in a shaky voice.

No answer. Should she look for him in his office? Or head back down to concessions and leave a note that she was quitting?

A faint crash came from Mark's office. What if he had a heart attack and fell over? He looked ill at their meeting earlier. Erin didn't want to walk down the dark hallway again, but she didn't want to leave Mark in trouble. Henry wasn't dependable. Maybe he left early and let the computer take care of itself.

Erin brought her phone out. If she had to call to Siri for help, she'd be ready, phone in hand. One of the bulbs in the overhead fixture had burned out, making the shadows loom larger than before. She cautiously made her way, heart pounding a heavy metal drum solo in her chest. A jumble of electrical cords just inside the office door threatened to wind itself around her ankle like vipers in a snake pit.

Mark's office was abandoned. A plastic bin that held the movie tickets was overturned, the tickets strewn about the desk. The drawers of the two old filing cabinets hung open, papers heaped on the floor. Black horn rim glasses lay on the floor next to Mark's empty chair. A faint whiff of smoke drifted across the room from the direction of the old balcony that overlooked the early theater.

Was it too cold for Barb to smoke outside? Maybe she

moved indoors to enjoy her cigarette in comfort.

She called again, "Barb? Mark? Anybody?"

The only answer was a hum from the big black box of the overhead electronics.

A whisp of smoke curled up from the balcony, weaving a dance through the black wrought iron bars. Mesmerized by the mysterious smoke, Erin shuffled toward the propped open door and the rectangle of dim light.

She peered over the railing and saw tiny flames licking at the back of an upholstered seat. A small fire in a metal wastepaper can blazed between the curtained side wall and the last row of seats. The flickering flames threatened to travel down the ancient wood. Erin whipped up her cell to make a call.

She jabbed at the on button. "Siri, call 9…."

Before she could finish, a fist punch from behind knocked the phone from her grasp. It tumbled to her feet.

Erin twirled around screaming, "What the hell is wrong with you? I need to call 9-1-1. There's a fire down there!"

The man in the tan suit loomed before her, his brown Panama hat tilted sideways. An unearthly glow from his white mask repelled her. She tried to step away. The cold metal of the railing dug into her back. She couldn't take her eyes off the figure's face. The brown eyes staring back at her were definitely human, despite the ghostly countenance. Behind her the small fire on the theater floor was growing hotter.

***

Sandra barely slammed the door shut as Norm gunned the engine. The old Buick jumped into action. With a quick glance over his shoulder, Norm shot into the street. Luckily, no cars were behind him as he drove ten, then fifteen miles over the speed limit. The stoplight by Literatus was green as they roared past, the grandmother with the child still in her arms glared at them.

However the light at the intersection before the Classic was turning yellow. Norm glanced right, then left as he zoomed through the red light. He came to a screeching halt, jumped the curb and smashed into the bench in front of the Classic.

Gaston was frantically howling and scratching at the closed door of the cinema. His front claws etched a mark on the glass surface. Norm leapt out of the car and heaved open the door. The poodle raced into the lobby with Norm close behind. Sandra scurried as fast as her wobbly legs could move, fearful of what they might find inside the theater. Gaston never acted with such ferocity unless there was trouble.

The pooch disappeared up the steps. Norm thundered at his heels. Sandra sniffed the air. A faint odor of smoke wafted down the hallway from the old theater. She froze, torn between pursuing Gaston and Norm up the stairs and checking out the source of the smoke.

***

"Who…who are you? What do you want?" Erin said with a tremor in her voice

"I warned you to stop snooping. I heard you and the old busybody meddling in the old apartment."

"You're the one who left behind the Coke can and the bee cage!"

"Ah, the bee cage. I had the fool proof murder. Victoria was the perfect victim. All I had to do was trap some bees in a cage. Give it a little shake. They took care of the rest."

"But why?"

"Let's just say she was a lifelong enemy. She ruined my life, so I set out to ruin hers."

The figure took a menacing step closer, hands ready to throttle anyone in his reach.

Erin looked frantically around for help. "What did I ever do to you?"

"You're in the wrong place at the wrong time. You're going to have an unfortunate accident, too. A tragic fall over the balcony, then an equally tragic fire. The old theater always was a fire hazard. Look at all the flammable trash up here." The man gestured at the debris heaped up on every spare surface.

"What about Mark? He'll know something was wrong."

"He's about to perish in the out-of-control fire, too."

'What about Barb?

"She fortunately went home before the blaze started?"

"And Henry?"

"Who do you think told Barb to knock off early? Who's spreading the fire? Enough talk."

The specter grabbed her shoulders and roughly shoved her

backwards over the balcony. Erin grasped the metal railing, and clung desperately to the cold iron. The twisted metal dug into her hands. She turned her head and bit the man on his exposed arm. *Definitely human.*

"You little bitch!" He loosened his grip with the injured hand. Erin could see the fury glinting in his eyes. She kicked his shin as hard as she could and screamed again.

"Help me. Somebody, please help!"

A frenzy of barking accompanied the ballistic missile of fur. Gaston torpedoed the man, sinking his sharp teeth into the gap between pant leg and athletic shoes with a low growl.

"Goddam dog!"

The man released Erin to ward off the canine attacker. He shook free from the dog's maw, and aimed a well-placed kick at his head. The poodle dodged the blow and continued his snarling assault. The two battled across the room, the man cursing as the dog darted forward and back, like Mohammed Ali's reincarnation. The hat flew off and a long ponytail flopped down.

Erin stooped down, her fingers seizing the top brick from the doorstop. She lunged forward, and raised the brick overhead. Using all her strength she struck the man's head with a sickening thump. The figure crumpled, and the mask slid down, revealing a decidedly feminine face.

"You're a woman!" Erin exclaimed. She knelt beside the inert body, the wound profusely bleeding. Gaston hunkered down, still growling low in his throat. A pool of blood began to accumulate under the woman's head.

She wrung her hands. "Oh, God. Did I kill her? Please don't let her die!"

Norm charged into the room and came to an abrupt halt when he saw the still figure and the girl's stricken face. "What's the hell's happening up here?"

***

The fire extinguisher on the wall. *That's it.* Sandra spurred into action, pulling it down in one swift motion. The canister was surprisingly light. She took a minute to study the pictured directions.

Pull pin. Squeeze lever. Hold upright. Aim.
Got it.

She dashed down the long hall as fast as her eighty-year-old legs could move, clutching the fire extinguisher as though her life depended on it. A flush of relief came over her when she arrived at the double doors of the old theater. Heeding the wall's warning to *watch out*, she maneuvered the uneven step down. The smoke was pouring from the rear. She saw the flames surging up from what looked like a trash can set afire.

Sandra hurried across the room. As she neared the site of the blaze, she nearly tripped on some jean clad legs sprawled between the seats. At first she thought the quirky manager had dressed the mannequin torso. To her shock, she realized it was an unconscious Mark, his leg twisted into an awkward angle.

No time to stop and render aid. She had to put out the fire first.

With shaking hands, she inserted a trembling finger into the red circular pin and pulled it out, holding the canister as upright as she could manage. Then she squeezed the lever with one hand while holding the nozzle with the other, targeting the base of the fire with the stream of chemicals. Whoosh! She pressed the lever tightly as the spray jetted out.

A gangly man holding a red gas can stepped out of the shadows. "What do you think you're doing?"

"I'm putting out this fire. What does it look like?"

"No you're not. Take your hands off the fire extinguisher or I'll soak you with this gas. I've got a full gallon. You'll light up like Joan of Arc." He advanced closer, aiming the yellow spout at her.

"I don't think so." Sandra shifted the spewing flame retardants in his direction.

He dropped the canister and clutched his eyes, screaming, "You crazy bitch! You sprayed that shit in my eyes!"

Sandra went back to dowsing the flames. Soon the fire sputtered out.

Suddenly she heard a voice from above. "What's going on down there?"

She looked up to see Norm standing on a small balcony framed in a patch of light. Gaston stuck his nose through the black railings and barked before running back into Mark's office.

"I just put out a fire and took care of the fire starter." She pointed to the groaning man. "He threatened to turn me into Bananas Foster! What are you doing up there?"

"Erin just knocked out the man in the tan suit. Maybe Victoria's murderer. Only it ain't a man. She's worried about Mark. Have you seen him?"

"He's down here—unconscious. I didn't have time to check on him but I will now. But there's more."

The moaning man was inching his way toward the double doors. His countenance was an angry red, already starting to blister. "Water! Get me to the rest room where I can splash some water on my face."

"We need your help," Sandra said. "The arsonist is complaining about his face. I still haven't seen to Mark."

"Be right down. I called 9-1-1. The cops are on the way."

Chapter Thirty-Four
The Case Gets Cracked

Tears streaming down her cheeks, Erin raised her head and pleaded, "Uncle Norm. Please do something. He... I mean she tried to push me off the balcony. Then Gaston saved me." The poodle barked in agreement. "But I hit her hard. I think I killed her."

Norm bent down and picked up the woman's wrist. "She still has a strong pulse. She's not dead. But she'll probably have a hell of a headache."

He gathered the weeping girl in his arms. "It will be OK." He gently patted her back. "Don't cry. The EMT's will take care of her."

He stood up and dialed the emergency number. "We have an unconscious woman at the Classic Cinema. A head injury. Second floor. Door's open. Better send the police too. It's part of a murder investigation."

"I gotta look what's going on down there," Norm said, heading toward the balcony, as Gaston flitted beside him "Ya gonna be all right?"

The girl tearfully nodded. She stood staring at the woman, lips tightly compressed. She wrapped her arms around herself in a little hug.

Norm shouted down to Sandra, "Be right down. I called 9-1-1. The cops are on the way."

He returned to Erin, reluctant to leave her alone. Gaston rubbed against her ankles, then plopped down at her feet.

"Ya sure yer OK? Sandra needs me downstairs. The cops should be here any minute."

The woman on the floor gave a little moan as her eyes fluttered open. She reached her hand to the back of her head and brought it up to her face, staring in disbelief at the smear of blood. She groaned loudly, dropped her hand down, eyes closing again.

"The EMT's will be here soon. So will the cops, so don't try any funny business," Norm said to the woman. He gave Erin a little hug. "Gotta go, Darlin'. Gaston will protect you."

"Thanks, Uncle Norm." She dropped down to pat Gaston and he licked her salty face.

Then her phone rang. Erin scrambled across the floor to retrieve it. Vlad didn't even wait for her to speak. "Where are you? Your mother asked me to pick you up. I've been waiting on Fourth Street for almost a half hour." Erin could hear the sounds of sirens in the background. "An ambulance is headed your way. Don't tell me you're hurt?"

"I'm OK," Erin reassured him. "But Mark's been hurt. Auntie Sandra and Uncle Norm are downstairs taking care of things."

"Where are you?"

"I'm upstairs in Mark's office."

"I'm on my way." She listened to the slam of the car door and her dad's curses as he rushed toward the theater.

Erin looked again at the woman on the floor and told her dad, "We caught the man in the tan suit. Only it's not a man."

"What are you talking about? The man in the tan suit? I knew your mother shouldn't have let you go in tonight," Vlad said angrily.

The phone clicked off. Erin heard the pounding of the EMT's as they came up the stairs, down the hall, and rushed into the room wheeling a stretcher. The burly one dropped to his knees to examine the woman's bleeding head. He reached inside his bag for a scissors and cut away the white Phantom mask, tossing it aside.

"Was this some costume party that got out of hand?" the man asked, placing his fingers on each side of her head with his thumbs up. "Size it for three fingers."

The rangy EMT brought out a blue and yellow collar, lined up some holes, and knelt down beside the larger man. As the first EMT gently held the woman's head, the second man slipped the contraption around her neck and fastened it with a Velcro strap. "How did this happen?" he asked.

Erin answered in a small voice, "She tried to push me over the balcony and Gaston bit her. Then I hit her with a brick."

Gaston barked at the mention of his name. The two men carefully moved the stretcher next to the injured woman.

Hot on their heels, Vlad burst into the room and gathered Erin in a tight hug. "Are you all right, Sweetheart?"

She buried her head in his shoulder and tearfully nodded. "I was afraid she was going to kill me. There was a fire down in the theater. I heard Auntie Sandra put it out."

Just then a huge man lumbered into the room. "I might have known you'd be here," he said in a gravelly voice. "I suppose Sandra Tooksbury is around here somewhere. Wherever the poodle shows up, his owner can't be far behind."

"Detective Johnson, I believe you've met my daughter." Vlad nudged Erin in the policeman's direction. "She can explain better than I what's going on."

The large EMT spoke to the detective, "We're taking this woman to the emergency room. Do you want to meet us there?"

Detective Johnson studied the woman's face for a few seconds. "She looks familiar. I've seen her face in the news a while ago. Disappeared in Lake Superior."

Norm entered the room and spoke to the EMT's. "I got another one for you in the men's room. He got sprayed in the face with fire retardant. Seems the two of them were going to burn down the Classic."

"Take him along to the hospital with you, I'll be along in a minute," Detective Johnson said.

"Ya might need to make room for three. Sandra's downstairs with the theater manager. He just came to. It looks like his leg is broke pretty bad."

"We'll get another ambulance over here," the large EMT said. "Isn't that dog the one that brought down the killer at the fitness center? We were there when the old lady called Med-Alert."

"And when you got attacked at Tripoli Island," said his partner. "Nice to see you again, Dr. Chomsky. We carried you off the island. That dog sure gets around."

The woman moaned from the stretcher. The EMT's moved her swiftly toward the door.

"You better get going." Detective Johnson growled. "Just let me finish up here." He pulled up Mark's office chair and gestured for Erin to sit down. Then he cleared off the other chair and sat on it. Vlad stood behind Erin, hands on her shoulders, and gave her a reassuring squeeze as she related the events of the evening to the policeman. Gaston joined in with an occasional yip.

"You're a very lucky young lady. The whole thing could have gone terribly wrong," the policeman scolded. "When you saw the writing on the wall, you should have immediately left the building and called the police."

The girl hung her head. "I know. I wasn't thinking. My mom told me to call at the first sign of trouble. Only I wanted to tell Mark."

"Next time you hopefully will make better choices. It's our job to protect people. Never be afraid to call us." He stood up and said to Vlad. "Can you please bring her down to the station tomorrow? We'll need her statement. Bring Mrs. Tooksbury and that handyman of hers, too. We'll sort this all out in the morning. I'm sure it has to do with Victoria Fitzgerald's murder."

"Of course. Anything to help."

The detective muttered under his breath, "If you really wanted to help, you'd all move to a different state."

"Let's check on Norm and Auntie Sandra," Vlad said. "and figure out how we're going to explain this to your mother."

***

"Thank God, today's Saturday," Vlad said. "I couldn't have faced my seven-thirty lecture after the night I had. If Maria had a brick handy, I might be getting stitches in my head, too." He sank down into Sandra's overstuffed couch and nervously pulled on his mustache.

Beatrice placed a comforting hand on his leg. "At least none of us were hurt. Erin was a very courageous girl!"

The four friends gathered at Sandra's apartment for an armchair analysis of the previous night's discoveries. Sandra stood in front of the small liquor cabinet shaking up martinis, while Norm helped himself to a beer in the kitchen. Only Gaston wasn't partaking of a celebratory beverage. Instead he was snoozing in his sheepskin dog bed strategically placed in the sunniest spot in the living room.

Sandra filled three martini glasses, shuffling over to Vlad and Beatrice with two. Then she settled into her recliner and said, "I called Robert Doering this morning and told him we solved the case—with a little help from Erin."

Norm plopped next to Vlad, beer in hand. "Ya got yerself

quite a little pistol there. She beaned that babe with a brick before I made it up the stairs.”

“She must have been so frightened,” Beatrice shook her head. “Imagine confronting a ghost and a killer.”

“Lucky that Gaston arrived in the nick of time!” Sandra said. “I misjudged the poor pooch. I thought he was running away to Literatus for a treat. But he sensed Erin was in danger. I told that detective he was psychic!”

“Vlad got a call from Detective Johnson this morning,” Beatrice said. “It was a complete surprise.”

“Did he want to charge ya with obstruction?” Norm asked.

“Not at all.” Vlad smiled at the group. “He acted like a real human being. He was worried about Erin and wanted me to tell her Mark was going to be fine. He had a bad break and will need surgery to put pins in place.”

“Did he tell you anything about the so-called ghost and that maniac with the gas can?” Sandra asked.

“The arsonist was Henry Radke, the projectionist. The man in the tan suit was really a woman, Liz Lederman.”

“The woman who committed suicide? Whose body was never found in Lake Superior?” Sandra shook her head in disbelief.

“That’s the one.” Vlad snapped his fingers. “She and Henry devised the whole scheme for revenge on the Fitzgerald’s. She faked her death so no one would suspect her of murder. They knew about the old apartment on the second floor and figured it was a perfect hide out for what they were planning.”

“Why dress up like a ghost?” asked Beatrice.

“Staff at the Classic claimed to have seen a man in a tan suit for years. That rumor played right into their plot to kill Victoria and make people believe the theater was cursed. Scare them into staying away.”

“It almost worked. Erin had me believing she’d seen a ghost,” Sandra said.

“Liz got the idea to write the fake letter luring Victoria to the movie. Everyone knew of her severe allergy. Henry occasionally worked for a beekeeper who taught him how to trap bees in the cage. He let Liz sneak into the theater with a few bees. She stole Victoria's purse while she was engrossed in the movie. During the loudest part of the film, she turned the bees loose and they did the rest. Liz disappeared out the back door. Everything was going as planned until Gaston found the bee cage."

"OK, I understand the revenge bit, but why the fire?" Norm looked puzzled.

"The theater owner at the mall wanted to close down the Classic for years, but Mark kept it afloat. Then Henry got the idea to burn it down for money, so he made a deal with the mall owner. He and Liz would take the cash and run. Start a new life somewhere else. Only they didn't count on Mark getting suspicious. When he confronted Henry about his strange behavior, the two men argued. Liz appeared in her tan suit disguise and shoved Mark over the balcony."

"So now what?" Norm asked

"The other theater owner is in big trouble—being charged as an accessory to arson. Henry and Liz are in the county jail waiting to meet with their lawyers."

"At least they're getting their wish for a new life—only it's in prison," Beatrice wryly observed.

"It's just like the story I heard on the news yesterday," Norm said. "This factory in Milwaukee that made frozen Chinese dumplings suffered the worst case of arson in recent history. Supposedly the work of a disgruntled employee."

"Did he use his "fire" arm?" Vlad snickered using his fingers to make quotation marks.

"Nope. But the police chief said it was the worst case of wonton destruction he'd ever seen."

The peals of laughter woke Gaston. He jumped off his dog bed and zoomed around the room, yipping excitedly. After a few laps about the living room, the pooch slammed on the brakes in front of Norm and moved into his begging posture.

"Ya got any Pork Chomps for the poor little fella? He deserves a treat for all his hard work."

"I think we all do. Your joke made me hungry for Chinese food. Let's order take out from the Bamboo Kitchen. My treat for a job well done," Beatrice offered.

"Sandra's martinis and chicken fried rice. I can't think of a better ending to a tough case." Vlad set his empty glass on the cocktail table and extended a hand to Beatrice. "I'll drive."

Sandra ambled over to the leash hanging on a hook near the door. "Better add some sesame chicken. Gaston loves a little Chinese."

Chapter Thirty-Five
Twice Bitten

On a golden Saturday in October, the kind where summer refuses to loosen its grip on the temperature, Erin walked the two miles to the Classic Cinema. Both her mom and dad offered to drive her, but she wanted to enjoy the balmy eighty-degree weather. It would be six months before Wisconsinites would see a heat wave like this again. Deep purple asters and bright yellow mums were blooming in the yards, signaling fall was on its way, but Erin refused to play along, instead wearing shorts and an anime t-shirt.

Besides, she needed the time alone to ponder what her school counselor had told her during their last appointment. "You are not what happened to you. You can't change all the events from that night. But you can decide not to be triggered by them." When Erin felt her anxiety building up inside her, uncontrolled images of the man—no Liz, the woman—pushing her over the railing, she tried to go to a place of calm. She practiced the deep breathing the counselor taught to reach her inner blue sky, where the storm clouds of fear and anger passed by.

"Let it go," she told herself. Dancing, gymnastics, swimming, any physical activity helped to push out the angry thoughts. *I hate those assholes for hurting Mark and for threatening Auntie Sandra. Henry almost burned down the damn theater.* But they were in jail now. She was safe from them and determined to enjoy this walk to work. Her mother and father told her she could quit working at the Classic, but she argued. "If I quit, it means they win. I refuse to become a loser. Besides, Mark needs me especially now."

"I can't tell you how much I appreciate you coming in at the last minute," Mark said when she walked through the lobby. He pushed his walker behind the concessions counter. A cast went all the way from his knee to his hip. "Barb called in sick. I can't handle concessions by myself."

"It must be tough when you can't climb the stairs to the projection room and your office." Erin gave him a sympathetic smile. She carried boxes of candy out from the closet and began stocking the shelves.

Mark leaned on the counter as he reached under it for the sack of popcorn kernels. "The new projectionist is still feeling his way around. He had to carry the computer down here so I could show him how setting up the digital movie works. Luckily, he's a techie—caught on pretty quick."

"That's so dope! I mean, awesome," Erin crouched down to fill in the bottom shelf, arranging a row of Snickers next to the share size of M&M's. There were still plenty of Mike and Ike's on the middle shelf but only one box of Milk Duds remained.

"I'll call him, ask him to come down so you two can meet." Mark whipped out his cell phone and tapped on a name. "Hey, Steve. C'mon down. Erin's here. You know, the girl with the dog who saved the theater."

Erin blushed as she said, "It was Gaston and Auntie Sandra who did most of the work. In fact, Gaston rescued me!"

"That's why I gave them both a free lifetime pass to the movies. And all the popcorn the pooch can eat."

Erin heard the footsteps clumping on the stairs, but she wasn't expecting to see an incredible hottie suddenly appear at the bottom. His long wavy sandy-colored hair was swept to the side revealing smoldering hazel eyes and thick dark eyelashes. Almost perfect nose and lips like a young Brad Pitt. Even his loose-fitting Crawford U t-shirt couldn't hide his chiseled chest and arms. She almost dropped the box of Mild Duds at the sight of his biceps. *Wow! He's rizz! I'm glad I said yes when Mark called. Coming to work will be lit!*

"Erin, meet Steve Saunders, our new projectionist. He's a sophomore at Crawford. This is Erin, my right-hand girl." Mark's eyes twinkled with amusement at Erin's raised eyebrows and dropped jaw.

"So glad to finally meet you," Steve said as he flashed his smile exposing perfect white teeth. "Both Mark and Barb have been telling me about you."

Erin quickly recovered her composure. "It's nice to meet you, too." She stared a second longer at his dreamy eyes, then hastily added, "How do you like working here so far?"

"It's great. The perfect job. I can go to my classes during the day and work here at night. Plus I get to see all the movies. Once he's able to navigate the stairs, Mark says I can cut back on some of the hours."

"Yeah, it must be hard to do both work and school full time." Erin tried to act nonchalant. "I like just working part time. I still get to see more movies than my friends."

"It's OK." Steve shrugged. "Right now I can use the money."

"Me too. I'm saving for a car. Once I get my license, I plan on driving to school and volleyball practice. Maybe head to Milwaukee for some concerts." She bent down to finish stocking the row of candy.

"Is everything going all right upstairs?" Mark paused setting up the popcorn maker to give Steve his undivided attention. "Any questions?"

"No, it's a piece of cake. You programmed everything exactly. I'll be able to do it myself once I get the hang of it." Steve hesitated, then said, "But there is something I wanted to ask you about?"

"What is it?" Mark turned back to measuring popcorn.

"I heard a noise in the hallway, like footsteps. I knew it couldn't have been you obviously. You said Barb wasn't coming in. The footsteps kept coming closer and closer. I was really busy going over the schedule so I just shouted, "Come on in." I figured maybe you sent a friend up to check on me, but nobody came to the door."

"Huh?" Mark muttered, setting down the plastic cup. Erin's eyes grew wide.

"There was a thump like something got knocked over, so I got up to check it out. When I looked down the hall, I saw some guy, all dressed up in a suit. Standing in front of the old storeroom. The one with Chewbacca in front of it."

Mark and Erin froze. They stared into each other's eyes.

"A man in a tan colored suit?" Scarcely able to breathe, Erin somehow got the words out.

"Yep, that's what he was wearing. Old fashioned, slicked back hair, like out of the 1940's. I thought maybe he was an actor from the Crawford Players scoping out the theater. When I asked, "How may I help you?" He kind of vanished." Steve wore a puzzled expression as he glanced from Mark to Erin.

"Um… uh… well," Mark hemmed and hawed. "Sometimes we do let the Crawford Players use the theater for an event, but not recently."

"That's weird. I could have sworn he was dressed like a character from some play."

"And he didn't say anything?" Mark asked.

"Nope. Just stood there next to Chewbacca." Steve's forehead wrinkled in concentration. "At least I thought I saw a guy in the shadows."

Erin tittered behind her hand, then said. "Probably it's just your imagination. The mind can play tricks on you in an old theater."

Acknowledgements

First to the readers of my books: I am highly motivated by your feedback and kind comments to continue writing even when my "pen" runs dry. I'm so happy to be able to answer your question, "are you writing another book?" with a resounding YES. Thank you.

I am also blessed to belong to a most excellent writers' group on zoom. Our weekly meetings provide a deadline to avert any chronic procrastination. Your insightful comments and generous sharing of your talents is much appreciated. Thank you, Sherri A. Lynn, Wendy Wyatt, and of course, Karen Hodges Miller.

This book would not have been possible without your help.

Karen Hodges Miller provides the inspiration and wisdom that writers need. She is a gifted editor whose influence goes beyond the written word. Successful writers are not the ones who craft a good sentence. They are the ones who keep writing. Karen motivates her colleagues to never give up.

To the incredible Eric Labacz, who has designed all the covers of my cozy mysteries, thank you. Your talents as an artist are exemplary. You have an intuitive grasp of my stories and capture both the humor and menace.

My long-standing Watertown writers' group started me on this path and still walk along beside me on this journey. Fran Milburn, John Aschenbrenner, Paul Marose, Kay Ferguson, Bruce Benz and Mike Kujawa, thank you for your support and suggestions.

A very special thanks goes to Matt Hanson of the Towne Cinema. From the moment I walked out of the dark theater where a total of five moviegoers watched *Poor Things*, and told Matt, "I have an idea for a murder mystery," he has been an enthusiastic supporter. He met me at the Towne so I could explore the spooky upstairs and shared the legend of the man in the tan suit.

Even when he felt sick, he still opened up the Towne so I could get more pictures to send to Eric.

I'd also like to thank Beth Boxell for her advice on popcorn makers, Dan Ludwig, for his bee keeping knowledge, and the owners of the two dogs in my life: Stella who belongs to Chris and Heather Detrie and Emmy, owned by Robert and Joyce Herald. There's a bit of each of them in Gaston.

I appreciate my daughter, Megan, for her knowledge of writing and editing. Our "brief but spectacular" discussions sustain my writerly life. Most of all, I'd like to thank my husband, Michael, for his unwavering support, his practical suggestions, and his good judgement of when to disappear to let me write undisturbed. Your belief in my writing is only overshadowed by your love!

A special acknowledgement goes to my departed sister, Judy. Every Friday morning when I visited, her first question was "how's the book coming?" I miss her sharp sense of humor and her listening ear more than words can express. She's gone home to Jesus –a final victory.

About the Author

Janice Detrie lives with her husband in Watertown, Wisconsin, which bears a strong resemblance to the fictional Crawford. A retired literacy coordinator, she loves reading all types of books, especially a good (cozy) mystery, and stories with a few twists. Most days she can be found seated at her computer, writing or procrastinating about writing. Her hobbies include making jewelry, Zumba-ing, shopping at thrift stores and anything that gets her away from housework. She has two children and three grandchildren.

You can find her on BookBub, Amazon, Facebook and Goodreads. To read her blogs and see an interview, visit her website at janicedetrie.com

Other Books in
the Gaston the Poodle
Series

The 7-10 Split

A Glint in Her Ice

Murder is as Easy as Pie

To Die for Pickleball